RUN WITH MY HEART

A Christian Christmas Football Romance

LORANA HOOPES

To my wonderful readers who inspire me to write everyday.
To my father who got me into watching football when I was young.
To Emmitt Smith who was my favorite ball player of all time. He
had so much class, and I loved how he finished his degree as well.
Such an inspiration!

Tucker Jackson's blood boiled as he watched the seconds on the clock run out. The buzz of the clock felt like a nail straight to his heart as did the cheers from the other team's fans. Three points. Just three measly points. How could they have gotten so close? They had tasted the victory and then lost it.

An urge to hit something surged within him, and he curled his hand into a fist to keep it at bay. He thought he'd quelled the angry beast that lived inside of him with his boxing classes. Boxing classes that his friend and former teammate Emmitt Brown had recommended when his anger had surfaced because of the trade. And they'd been helping. Five days a week of pounding a bag was generally enough to appease the hunger. So, anger wasn't usually his go-to emotion anymore, but *this* was ridiculous.

This was their second loss in a row, and both were by fewer than ten points. Sure, this was the toughest part of the team's schedule. The teams they were playing now had good records, but the Tornadoes did too. At least they had. If they continued playing like this, they would lose their spot in the playoffs. With this loss, they were now sitting in the wild card position. Which meant that instead of a week off to recover, they had to play in the wild card game and win to move to the quarterfinals. One more loss, and they would be out. Their season would be over. They had to win the next game.

And the next game was on Christmas Day just ten days away. Not the best day to play a football game. Morale was always a little lower because the men wanted to be with their families, especially the men with kids. Tucker didn't have any kids, and he wasn't that close to his family anymore, but he didn't enjoy playing on Christmas Day either. Christmas Day was for watching silly holiday movies and eating too much.

He took off his helmet, clenching it in his left hand, as he joined the line of his teammates. It was tradition after every game to slap hands with the opposing team members. It was supposed to encourage camaraderie and discourage fighting, but Tucker wasn't sure how effective it was. Maybe in high school when their jobs and paychecks hadn't been on the line, but this was pro-football. How much money the team paid you depended on individual playing time during the games and team performance throughout the season, so every play mattered. Every game mattered. And slapping hands with the men who had just lowered your paycheck often felt unnatural and forced.

Tucker kept his eyes down as he made his way through the line. "Good game. Good game." The rote words rolled off his tongue without a conscious thought as his mind wandered back to the trade that had landed him here. Last year at this time, he had been on the Rebels. Sure, he hadn't gotten to play as much, but the Rebels had won the Championship game. He even had the ring to prove it, although it meant less than it might have because he'd known even then he was getting traded to the Texas Tornadoes.

Trades happened in football. All the time. But why did it have to happen to him? He'd always been one of the best - in high school, in college, but he hadn't even gotten the chance to show the Rebels what he could do. And yes, the Tornadoes were letting him run more, but what good was that if they didn't win? Perhaps, if the Rebels saw how good he was, they might trade for him back, but even that was a shot in the dark. Had a team ever done that? He didn't know.

With the obligatory congratulatory line finished, he headed toward the locker room. Blaine Hollis, quarter-back, captain, and longest team member stood at the door smiling and patting the guys' shoulders as they entered. Blaine was the definition of good sportsmanship. In fact, Tucker was fairly certain his face would be next to the word in the dictionary. Win or lose, the man always had a smile and an encouraging word. Most days, Tucker found it refreshing - it reminded him of his former teammate Emmitt who everyone had called "Rev" - but not today. Not after losing a game they should have won.

"Good game." Blaine nodded and clapped Tucker on the shoulder. "We'll get them next time." Hollis was a good guy, but he was always spouting platitudes like these. Platitudes that felt empty when the loss column rose in number instead of the win column. Tucker was tired of his optimism. Optimism and platitudes didn't win championships.

"Will we?" Tucker asked. The condescension in his voice surprised him. He wasn't normally so pessimistic, but he hadn't adjusted to Southlake the way he thought he would have by now. People had flocked to him in the past, but he was beginning to wonder if that had been more because of his family's money than himself.

His father was a prominent attorney in San Antonio, and he had donated a lot of money to buildings and charities to get his name on things - a dormitory hall, a high school stadium, a hospital wing. The fame benefited Tucker, and he had never lacked for anything in his life, except maybe a father who was physically there. However, he was not experiencing the same thing here. Not that the people weren't nice, it was just that they were also like him. He didn't stand out. Not like he used to. "If we lose the next game, we're out for the rest of the season. If you had just let me run that last play…"

Blaine shook his head and fixed his steely eyes on Tucker. His voice dropped to his serious captain's tone - the one that declared he was in charge, and he would not allow backtalk. "I made a call. They were all over your running game today. Maybe it would have played out differently if you had run but maybe not. We can't win every game, Tucker, and if you only focus on the ones we lose, you will never find the joy of playing the game."

The joy of playing the game? This wasn't some neighborhood tackle game. This was his livelihood Blaine was being so blase about. "Is that what you guys told yourselves when you lost last year?"

Tucker stared defiantly at Blaine. He knew Blaine wasn't to blame for the Tornadoes' losses last year; he was a good quarterback. In the top five of the league to be exact. The problem was that there were thirty-two teams and only two made it all the way to the championship game, so sometimes being good wasn't good enough. Still, he couldn't seem to tame the anger coursing through his veins.

"Shower and get out of here," Blaine said with a nod toward the locker room behind him. "You need some time off." Though his words were forceful, and his level gaze backed them up, he didn't raise his voice or yell. Tucker might have felt better if he had. The quiet, even tone reminded him of his mother's scolding when he'd been in trouble growing up; and just like then, it quelled Tucker's anger and made him realize his mistake.

"Blaine, I'm sorry, man. I'm just frustrated." Tucker knew he had stepped over the line, and if he didn't get back in Blaine's good graces, he'd be riding the bench and probably facing another trade. In fact, if he didn't watch it, he'd wind up with a label on his back that would make every team in the league shy away from him. And then where would he be?

"We all are, but I wasn't kidding. Go clear your head and decide if this is still *where* you want to be, *what* you want to be doing. IF it is, I'll see you at practice at noon tomorrow."

Tucker knew better than to argue. Like a scolded puppy, he hung his head and shuffled past Blaine, barely managing a "Yes, sir." He berated himself as he walked to his locker. His temper was getting the better of him. Again. And he needed to get it under control. This was a struggle he thought he had won but apparently not.

Around him, the banter from his teammates created a soft buzz. A few words bypassed the static and reached his ears - favorite plays of the game, mistakes they'd made. How did they all appear in better spirits than Tucker?

Why did he let his frustration get the better of him? Why did he always focus on the worst-case scenario?

Shelby Doll sighed as she watched Quinn attempt to dribble a basketball and give up when the ball refused to bounce. She had already put air in the ball twice this week, but it seemed to lose the air as soon as she filled it. Just another thing she needed to replace if she only had the money.

"Uh oh, I know that sigh," her friend Kenzi said beside her. "What's wrong?"

"What's always wrong?" Shelby didn't know why Kenzi even asked. It was always the same answer. "Money. The rent is due on this place by the end of the month, and we don't have it. Attendance has dropped since that trampoline park opened up down the street."

She didn't want to wish ill on any business, but that place was the bane of her existence. They'd come in a few months ago with flashy signs, a new sparkling building, and more money to spend on advertising and specials than she'd make in a year. The town of South-lake was rather affluent, and most families had been using the community center because it was the only option. When the trampoline park opened, those that had the money to spend had pulled their kids, leaving the few kids who were already scraping by as the only customers.

"That place is just a fad," Kenzi said with a wave of her hand. The sparkly pink of her nails caught the light and sent tiny rainbows of colors dancing across the nearby wall. Kenzi always had her nails painted, and it changed with her mood or her outfit. Shelby, on the other hand, rarely painted her nails, and when she did, it was never a frivolous red or a fluffy pink color. A clear polish was much more functional.

"It won't last," Kenzi continued, "and when kids tire of it, they'll come back here because you are amazing." She flashed her famous cheerleader smile - the one that had made her one of the most popular girls in college - as she squeezed Shelby's shoulder.

Shelby didn't know about that. When she took over managing the center a year ago, she felt amazing, but now she felt... behind the times. "What if they don't? Those kids out there need us." Her eyes found Darby, the young girl with glasses bigger than her face whose father had just been killed in the line of duty. Her mother needed this place for Darby, but she was strapped financially now that she was a single mother. And then there was Quinn. Tall and skinny, kids often picked on him at school because he spent more time reading than playing sports or the newest video game. But here he was just one of the gang. His mother was battling cancer, so there was no extra money there. And there was Benji. She still wasn't sure exactly how he had become paralyzed as he never talked about it, but his father had left when he was young, and his mother worked long hours.

There were other kids, but these three always stood out to her because they seemed to need the center the most. She scanned the gymnasium again. Once, they had watched nearly every school age kid in town for at least a few hours after school. Basketballs would echo across the floor as teams played. Others had staked one corner of the gym out for reading and playing cards. Still another part had been the creative hangout for students who enjoyed theater and role play. But then the trampoline park had opened and offered its flashy new entertainment for kids, and most of the kids had left.

Now, there were only a handful. A few basketballs still thudded against the floor, but even they sounded sad as if the kids couldn't muster the emotion of delight that had previously lived there. Now, most of the kids read or worked on homework, and the muted atmosphere broke Shelby's heart. Quinn placed the ball back into the rack and didn't even try another. He shuffled to the bleachers and sat down next to Darby.

"What if they don't?" she asked again. "What if, come the new year, we can't pay the rent, and we have to close the doors forever?" They had always run on a tight budget, but the drop in enrollment had quickly drained what little reserve they kept. If anything unexpected happened that they would have to repair, there would be no money. Plus, Christmas was right around the corner, and there would be little cheer at the center this year. There was no money for decorations, no money for a party, no money for gifts. Shelby pushed her wire-framed glasses up her freckled nose and sighed.

Kenzi flashed a sympathetic smile as she wrapped an arm around Shelby's shoulders. "We'll just have to pray that doesn't happen."

Prayer. Shelby knew how important that was; but while she would never stop praying, she couldn't stop the tiny voice that often whispered in her ear that she wasn't seeing her prayers answered yet. Was God even listening to her? Did He even care? Couldn't He send the money if He really wanted to? Drop a winning lottery ticket on the front doorstep? Or have a wealthy family leave a donation?

"I think we may need more than just prayers for help," Shelby said with a final glance at the gym. "We might need to pray for a miracle."

2

He shouldn't be here. He knew it, but he seemed incapable of keeping his feet from crossing the threshold into the dimly lit bar. No one even looked up as he pulled the door open, even with the gust of cold air that ushered him in.

Snow would hit their town soon. He could smell it when the wind blew - that cold, crisp scent that made plants curl up their roots and sink lower in the soil. The sharp bite in the air that seemed to gnaw through even the thickest jackets and sweaters to chill the bones. Snow didn't come often to Texas, especially not central Texas where the town of Southlake nestled between Keller and Grapevine, but the weather had been different this year. Colder, wetter, more extreme, and he felt that it would happen.

The acrid scent of cigarette smoke floated in the cloudy air as Tucker crossed the dingy floor to an empty barstool. An old country song crackled softly through overhead speakers that had seen better days. In fact, most of the interior of this place appeared to have seen better days. He wondered if the employees even noticed it anymore, but he doubted it. The one man he saw behind the bar wore an expression of boredom and acceptance as if this was good enough.

Tucker pulled out the barstool, unsurprised to see a rip in the upholstery. It fit his mood and mirrored the dilapidated feeling the rest of the place exuded, but for a reason he couldn't really explain, the cushion also held comfort. He abhorred finding comfort here, but he seemed incapable of changing it.

All he ever wanted was a relationship with his father; but because of his job, his father only seemed interested in two things - working and drinking. He wasn't an alcoholic by any means; but after working long hours, he would disappear to his study and nurse a beer. At least that was what he would do on the evenings he came home. Some nights, he hadn't even come home before Tucker and his sister had been asleep. So, Tucker had associated drinking with being close to his father. He only ever drank one; but while the frosty glass sat in front of him, he could pretend it was something they had in common, something they could bond over.

He hadn't always been this way. Tucker could remember a time when his father came home before dinner in the evenings, when he would scoop up Tucker and his younger sister and carry them around the living room under his arms like an airplane, when he would circle his arms around his wife's waist and kiss her neck as she tried to cook dinner, and she would playfully shoo him off. There was a time when laughter filled the house and a cheery glow surrounded the rooms, but all of that changed when his mother died.

He'd been in junior high then, worrying stupidly about acne and girls while a deadly tumor sprouted inside his mother's head. A tumor that grew tentacles and stealthily curled itself around different areas of her brain. A tumor none of them knew about until she died in her sleep one night. Tucker hadn't been the one to find her for which he had been grateful, but his father had. And it had changed him. Within a week, he stopped coming home for dinners. He hired a cook to take care of the meals for Tucker and his sister, Whitley. Occasionally, he would arrive home before they retired to bed, but more often than not, Tucker had been the one to make sure they did their homework and went to bed at a decent hour. In one week, he had basically lost both his parents and been forced to grow up faster than any teenage boy ought to. When other boys his age were worrying about homework and girls and the latest gaming system, he had been forced to worry about dishes and laundry and the well-being of his sister.

His father had poured money on them after that as if money could make up for the loss of their mother, or maybe he had done it in an effort to assuage his guilt for being gone so often. Either way, Tucker had hated that money. That money that replaced the one thing he really needed at the time - a parent. His anger had started about that time. Anger at the loss of his mother, anger at his father, anger at the money his father doled out instead of time.

Yes, the money had been the main target of his anger. Until it started opening doors for him. He had talent, but he was pretty sure it was his father's sizable donation that earned him a role on the Varsity football team as a fresh-man. Perhaps, he attained the title of captain of the team in his junior year (a title normally reserved for seniors and most often quarterbacks and not running backs) on his own, but it could have also been the new sports equipment his father provided even though he never attended a game. Then there was the full ride scholarship to a prestigious university that might have been based upon his talent or the amount of money his father had thrown to the program.

Either way, Tucker had enjoyed the benefits and the title of star running back for four years until he'd been picked up in the draft. His father's money had certainly paved the way for a cushy ride that may or may not have existed without it, and so Tucker had swallowed his angry feelings not realizing he was fostering their growth with his denial. It was only once he was on the Rebels roster that things had begun to change.

Being chosen in the draft had been a dream - one that he'd been pretty sure would happen - but a dream none-theless. However, when he'd arrived in the locker room the first day, he'd realized it wasn't the dream he had thought it would be. His father's money meant nothing here. Almost all of the players had come from money just like he had. Some even more, and some were legacy football players. Their fathers and grandfathers had played the game; so regardless of talent, they had found their way in.

That had been the hardest pill to swallow. He hadn't been signed as the main running back or even the backup running back. Instead, as a backup to the backup running back, he rarely got the chance to play in games, but he'd been sure once they saw his talent that would change. Except they'd traded him before he could prove himself, and now he was playing for a team who just couldn't seem to get their act together. And it was frustrating.

"Hey, you're Tucker Jackson, aren't you?"

Tucker glanced up at the man who belonged to the voice. He sat a barstool over and looked out of place in his expensive suit. Clearly a man who normally appeared well put together, he had obviously been served one too many as his voice held the slur of inebriation and red splotches dotted his face.

"No, man, you've got the wrong guy." Normally he enjoyed being recognized, even signing autographs for fans though some players hated it, but today he just wanted to nurse his wounded ego and dwell in the past.

"Yeah you are." The man stood, swayed on his feet momentarily, and then grabbed the bar to steady himself. His dress shirt hung out of his pants on one side and held the stain of whatever he'd eaten most recently. Still, he looked like a man who had money or wanted people to think he did. "You cost me a grand today."

Oh great. *This* he definitely didn't need. He knew people bet on sporting events even though it was illegal, but he'd never met anyone who actually did. Tucker imagined this man would be buying his beer had they won the game, but since they hadn't…. well, the man might be unsteady on his feet, but he looked solid and like an angry bull about to charge. Even as inebriated as he was, he might still be able to do some damage to Tucker. Damage that could keep him from playing in the next game.

"Look, man, I'm sorry you lost money, but betting on football is illegal." Tucker kept his voice neutral as he spoke and then returned his gaze to his drink. He hoped the man would take the hint and leave him alone. Unfortunately, either the man was stubborn or his good sense was clouded by liquor. Perhaps it was a combination of both.

An angry snort came out of the man's mouth and he shoved a pudgy finger in Tucker's face. "It wouldn't be an issue if you hadn't lost the game. Who taught you how to carry the ball anyway, your sister?"

Tucker tried to remain calm, but he'd never liked fingers shoved in his face; and he certainly didn't allow anyone to talk badly about his sister. He'd had to defend her all through school when her reaction to their mother's death had been to misbehave. Rumors had often circulated about her, and Tucker had squelched them one by one, usually through a nice payoff but occasionally with his fists when the perpetrator refused to let up. Fighting had been frowned upon in high school, but it was even more taboo in pro-football. A public fight could get you fined or suspended if anyone got hurt. Not to mention jail time if assault charges were filed.

"My sister is actually a pretty impressive running back," Tucker said in a last ditch effort to diffuse the man. Maybe he would take the joke and let it go.

"Then maybe they should hire her and let you go," the man said as he pushed Tucker's shoulder.

That touch broke the tenuous thread Tucker held on his anger. He slapped the man's hand away and jumped up from his barstool so quickly that it fell to the floor behind him. The loud bang of metal on the hard floor halted the conversation around them, and Tucker felt the eyes of the strangers on him. His hand shook as he forced it to his side. He couldn't punch the man now. Not here and certainly not with all these people watching. "I said let it go, man."

Having already paid for his beer, Tucker turned to leave. Regret that he hadn't been able to finish the drink in peace circled him like a cloud, but it paled in comparison to the regret he would face if he got suspended. His body still burned with anger, and he hoped the cool outside air would calm him down, but he never got the chance to see. Before he was halfway to the door, the force of something, or someone, knocked into him from behind, sending him careening into a table before forcing him to the floor. His breath rushed out in one gust as his ribs collided first with the sharp edge of the table and then with the hard floor. Then, he felt the pain as punches landed on his sides.

He rolled over, unsurprised to see the drunk man bending over him, but determined not to let the man beat him to a pulp. When his fist came close again, Tucker grabbed it and pulled. The sudden shift sent the man collapsing to the floor beside him, and Tucker let his own fists fly. He only meant to incapacitate the man long enough to get out of the bar, but once the first punch landed, he couldn't seem to stop the next one. Or the next one.

It was only the presence of an arm grabbing his, and

the pressure of a knee in his back forcing him to the floor that cleared his hazy red fog. "That's enough."

The voice was deep and unfamiliar, and Tucker twisted his head to see who it belonged to. The lone bartender stared back at him. He hadn't appeared threatening, but Tucker could feel the man's strength as he pinned Tucker's arms behind his back.

"It wasn't my fault. I tried to leave," Tucker said.

"I know. I saw it happen. Still had to call the police though. Have to report all fights that happen and file a report for the damages."

Tucker scanned the area and saw a broken chair and an upended table. "I can cover the damages."

"Sorry, it's the owner's rule, but I'll make sure they know you didn't start it."

Tucker wasn't sure that would matter to the team. It might keep him from getting officially charged, but he doubted the coach would just let this slide. Especially after his outburst at Blaine earlier.

Defeated, Tucker relaxed and waited for the cops to arrive, but when the cold metal snapped around his wrist, Tucker knew his worst fears had come true.

As Shelby watched a kid on a bicycle ride by outside the window, her thoughts turned again to the center. What

could she do to raise money and awareness? The annual
Christmas party often helped, but it wasn't enough and it
certainly wouldn't help this year if they couldn't find the
money to host it. Could they do a fundraiser? Possibly, but
what kind? It couldn't be anything that would cost the
families of the kids. They were the ones struggling already.
It would have to be something to reach the other members
of the community - either the ones who had stopped
coming or perhaps those who didn't even have kids but
could see the value of the place. The question was what
would that be?

"Shelby, can you come set the table?"

The voice of her mother calling from the kitchen
pulled her away from her plotting. With a sigh, she rose
from the couch and walked to the kitchen to grab plates
and silverware.

"Mom, do you know of any kind of fundraiser that
would get the community involved in donating to the
center?" Shelby asked as she pulled out the solid black
plates they used for everyday occasions. Her mother
owned China, beautiful china that she had been willed
when Shelby's grandmother died, but she only pulled it
out at Thanksgiving and Christmas. That gene of practi-
cality had trickled into Shelby as well although it had
morphed. She saw no use for the china even at holiday
dinners. Why have a set of plates you only used once or
twice a year? In her modest apartment, she had only one

set of plates and silverware, and they had been purchased on sale at Walmart. Of course, she also had no current need for china. Not with being a single woman who ate most dinners at her parent's house.

"Is money still an issue?"

Shelby chuffed out a breath. "When isn't it? The trampoline park drew most of our clients and the ones we have left can't afford a rate increase. I haven't even heard from the normal donors about the Christmas party yet, and at this point, I'm not sure we'll have the money to have one."

"Hmm." Her mother wasn't a business woman. She was a nurse, but she was still the smartest woman Shelby knew and she often had ideas that no one else thought of. "I assume you're thinking larger than a bake sale."

Shelby managed a slight chuckle as she pulled the silverware from the drawer and laid it on the top plate. "Yeah, I don't think baked goods are going to pull the kind of money we need."

"What about a celebrity? Someone who would draw in a different crowd." Her mother crossed to the island and retrieved a pot holder from the drawer.

"That's a great idea, but I don't know any celebrities. Kenzi might though. She's much more outgoing and maybe she has some connections. I could ask her tomorrow. What kind of celebrity are you thinking?"

Her mother shrugged. "I'm not sure it matters, but

isn't there a pro sports team housed around here somewhere?"

Shelby didn't watch sports, but it was her job to know the local businesses when she was canvassing for donations; and she knew there was a football team housed in Southlake. "There is a pro-football team, the Tornadoes I think, but what would a football player do at the center?"

Her mother picked up one of the pots and led the way to the dining room. "Well, he could talk to the kids about football, maybe teach them a few plays. Think of it like a learning clinic maybe or a gym class. People could pay to workout with him and possibly get an autographed ball or something."

Shelby's mother knew about as much about football as Shelby did, but what she was saying made sense. The wheels began turning in her head. "Yeah, that's a good idea. Even just having one of them signing merchandise for a small fee would bring in some money. I'll call tomorrow and see if any of them would like to come out and help. Hopefully, at least one of them has a good heart and some time because I have nothing to offer them in return."

Her mother set the pot on a heating pad in the middle of the table and turned to Shelby. "You have your amazing smile and heart for those kids. Any man should find that enough."

Shelby knew her mother was just being an encouraging mother, but the words reminded her instead of how she was still single. She knew it was just that she hadn't found the right man yet, but that didn't make her heartache any less real especially when it seemed someone from her high school was getting engaged every week. "Thanks, Mom. We'll see if you're right."

"I'm always right. Didn't you know that?" her mother said with a teasing smile. "Now, while I get the rest of the table ready, why don't you find everyone else and tell them dinner is ready?"

"Sure thing."

Dinner had always been family time in the Doll household. While everyone around them appeared to be drifting further apart, doing their own things, lost in their tablets and smartphones, her parents had been determined to keep them together. Because of that, dinner had been a sit down family affair when the family lived together even if they had often been passing each other at breakfast and eating lunch at different places altogether.

After Sam and Scott and finally Shelby moved out, the family still tried to eat dinner together as often as possible. And when Sam had married Iris, she had joined them as well. They couldn't come every night since they lived about an hour away, but they came as often as they could and always at least once a week.

Shelby always enjoyed the nights they came over. Not just because she loved seeing Sam, but she and Iris had formed a bond. Neither had a sister growing up; and like kindred spirits do, they had sensed that longing in each other and became fast friends.

Scott, like Shelby, was still single, but he would occasionally bring his flavor of the month over to meet the family. Their mother said he was just picky and that's why he dated so many different women, but Shelby was pretty sure Scott liked being single. Unlike herself.

She couldn't wait to start a family of her own, but being the quiet introvert she was, meeting men was hard, carrying on a conversation even harder, and forget asking a man out on a date. She'd rather have a root canal. So, she continued to pray about it, and every time she did, she felt God telling her to wait, that He had someone for her. She just wondered when her mystery man might show up.

Shelby found her father, brothers, and Iris in the main living room. The boys were arguing about some game on the TV and Iris was working a crossword puzzle. "Dinner's ready, guys. Mom made chicken alfredo."

Shelby wasn't sure they had Italian anywhere in their family, but somehow Italian dishes had always been the family's favorites and chicken alfredo topped that list. Especially when her mother made the alfredo sauce from scratch.

"Mmm, I do love Mom's chicken alfredo," Scott said as he and Sam rose from the couch. Iris stuck a pencil in her book, closed it, and set it on the table before joining them.

The savory smell of parmesan, cream, and chicken was strong as they entered the dining room. Shelby inhaled deeply and let the scent fill her nose and comfort her. There was something about Italian food that always made her feel... safe was a weird word, but it was as close as she could get.

For some reason, Italian food reminded her of simpler times. Times when her biggest worry was finding time to finish the new novel she had started or studying for the science test she hated, instead of trying to fund a community center and worrying about what would happen to the kids who needed the center if she couldn't get the money.

"Does anyone have anything we should pray over?" her father asked as he took his seat. His eyes travelled from one adult to the next.

"Shelby does. Go ahead and share, baby girl."

With a smile, Shelby squeezed her mother's hand. Though she was twenty-four and no longer a little girl, she didn't mind the nickname. Her mother had called her it for as long as she could remember.

"I could use prayer for the center. We're struggling financially right now, and I really need a miracle to keep the doors open."

"One miracle coming up." Her father's words held a teasing note, but Shelby knew he was serious. He had always believed in the power of prayer, always held on to the notion that God still provided miracles. When Shelby had asked one time why her prayer didn't get answered, he'd told her it had - just not in the way she'd expected. Shelby knew that if God didn't provide the funding for the center that her father would tell her perhaps God had something different planned for her. While she would accept that, she hoped that wasn't going to happen because the center wasn't just about her. It was about all those kids who needed a place to stay as well.

She closed her eyes and listened to her father's words, but even though she said 'amen' it didn't lessen the worry in her heart.

3

"Tucker Jackson?"

Tucker lifted his head at the sound of his name. The guard, a lithe man with a shaved head and more than a few tattoos who went by the name Mike, stood at the door of the jail cell. He looked much fiercer than he'd turned out to be - he'd checked on Tucker every half hour for the first few hours - but Tucker would still be glad when he was released and able to return home.

Sitting in a holding cell with three other men, one who reeked of alcohol and snored louder than a freight train, was not his idea of a good way to spend the night. Thankfully, the other two men hadn't seemed to know who he was and had left him alone. Even better, the man from the bar had been placed in a different holding cell, but Tucker was still very relieved to hear his name.

He stood, stretching his stiff legs, and crossed to the open door. "Thanks, Mike, my dad finally show up?" Tucker hadn't wanted to get his father involved, but better him than anyone on the team, so he'd used his one call to phone his father. Perhaps with his money, he could make the whole thing go away before anyone found out. He'd been working, of course, but had promised to do what he could.

The guard dodged his stare and shifted from one foot to the other. "Something like that." He blinked and Tucker noticed the back of his eyelids were tattooed as well. He couldn't imagine how painful that had been, and he wondered if Mike was just a sadist or if he had been using the pain from the needle to cover up some larger pain in his life.

Mike locked the cell door back and then led the way out to the processing area, but as the door opened and Tucker caught a glimpse of the figure waiting for him, his heart sank. It was not the stocky figure of his father, but the lean physique of Blaine Hollis waiting for him. How in the world had Blaine found out? And why was he here?

Tucker gathered his personal items, taking an extra moment to compose himself as he shoved his keys and wallet in his pocket, before turning to face Blaine.

"He all set?" Blaine asked Mike as if Tucker wasn't standing right next to him.

Mike glanced quickly at Tucker before dropping his gaze back to the counter. "Yes, sir, he's good to go."

"Good. Let's go, Jackson." Blaine headed for the exit without giving Tucker a chance to say anything. Tucker's stubborn streak wanted to refuse, to demand to know where his father was and why Blaine was here, but he could tell from the stiff set of the quarterback's shoulders that this was not the time nor the place. What could he say anyway?

The tense silence filled the space between them like some invisible third party as Tucker followed Blaine to his Ford Mustang. Red, yellow, and orange streaked the sky in a beautiful artistic pattern as the sun rose, but Tucker couldn't enjoy it. He was too worried about his future. Blaine unlocked the doors and motioned Tucker into the passenger seat, but he said nothing until they were both inside and the doors were closed.

"What were you thinking, Jackson?" Blaine's voice was low, but Tucker did not miss the anger that threaded it. "This isn't what I meant when I told you to think about your job."

"I wasn't trying to start the fight, Blaine." Tucker hated that he was having to defend himself to Blaine of all people. "I was trying to enjoy one beer. One. But then the man poked me and spouted off about my sister, so I got up to leave. He tackled me from behind, man. What was I supposed to do?"

"You're supposed to keep your cool," Blaine said in a tight voice. "We are in the public eye, Jackson, so everything we do is scrutinized. On top of that, our record isn't where our fans or the owners would like it to be. You may not like it or agree with it, but that puts added pressure on us. We can't afford any negative publicity right now. Not that it matters, but what was the fight about?"

Tucker shrugged, knowing his explanation changed nothing. "The guy was drunk and evidently he bet a grand we would win the game yesterday. Needless to say, he wasn't too happy we lost."

Blaine's sigh shook his broad shoulders, and he gazed out the windshield as if trying to think of what to say. Tucker took the opportunity to ask the question burning in his throat.

"Why are you here, Blaine? I called my father, not anyone from the team."

For just a moment, Blaine's jaw tightened, the muscles rippling beneath his skin. "Your father was buried in a case, Jackson. He couldn't make it, so he called Coach and Coach called me."

Disappointment blanketed Tucker's shoulders. His dad couldn't even find time to help out his son when he was in jail? He shouldn't be surprised; he couldn't remember the last time his father had been there when he needed him. "So, what's the verdict? Am I suspended?"

"No, not suspended. Your father may not have been able to be here, but he is still influential. Your charge was only going to be disorderly conduct anyway; but he got it dropped completely, so you wouldn't face suspension. However, you will have a hefty fine to pay, and we're going to have to find some way to improve your image in case this gets out. Some sort of community service."

"Community service?" Tucker exploded. "I was defending myself."

Blaine shot him a silencing look. "Community service is not negotiable. You have a chip on your shoulder, Jackson. It's affecting your game play, and now it's affecting the whole team. I don't know what your story is, but I think it's time you took a look at how the less fortunate live. Maybe that will give you some perspective."

Perspective. Blaine knew nothing about perspective. His father was probably in his life, and he probably attended every game Blaine had ever played. Tucker clenched his jaw to keep from saying the words rising in his throat. It would do no good to argue with Blaine right now. "What kind of community service and for how long?"

"I'm not sure yet. Coach and the public relations guy are going to look at some options. The judge didn't officially assign any, so that means they don't have to align it with the incident at the bar. This is more a requirement from the team. I'm sure it will be low key, but I would keep your evenings free. At least for the foreseeable future."

"What about practice? What about the next game?" This couldn't be happening. He hadn't started the fight. He'd tried to leave. Yes, he might have punched the guy one too many times, but he was only defending himself. Who could blame him?

"You'll still attend every practice and every game. The service will be done in your off time, and if you don't fulfill the time, then you will be suspended without pay for the remainder of the season. Should we happen to lose before the championship game, you will fulfill that suspension at the beginning of next season. Am I clear?"

"Crystal." Tucker said as he slumped against the seat. He should be grateful. It was better than being suspended, but giving up his evenings to do charity work was certainly not how he had planned to fill his time.

Shelby stared at the phone as she thought of what to say. How could she best convince the football team to send someone to help her out? She had nothing to offer in return besides the good karmic feelings of helping others out.

"You can't make the sell if you don't at least try," Kenzi said from behind her.

"I know, but what if they say no? Our usual donors have been so quiet this year. What if it stays like this? What if people are too busy or too focused on themselves to care about others? What if we're seeing the end of charitable donations?"

Kenzi's right eyebrow lifted as she chuckled. "Wow! Doomsday much? Seriously, you were made for this. Call them, tell them the amazing things you do, ask them for a player to hold a clinic or a signing or whatever. I'll bet you'll be surprised by humanity's response. I don't think we've completely fallen into the abyss yet."

"You're right," Shelby said with a shake of her head. She wasn't usually this dramatic, but it had just seemed the last few months that people cared less about the other people around them and more about their electronics. She'd seen more and more people scrolling their phones as they walked or during meals while others sat across from them, and their last fundraiser - a carwash in the summer - had been an absolute flop. People had said they were too busy to stop or that they'd come by later. Except they never had. The kids had been so disappointed. Shelby just didn't want to have to disappoint them again.

She took a deep breath and picked up the phone. She'd Googled the information for the team when she first arrived and had found the public relations manager's number. As her fingers pressed the buttons, she sent up a silent prayer for the right words to say.

The phone rang once, twice, three times in her ear. Disappointment pressed down on her shoulders, but just as she was about to hang up the phone, a voice answered.

"Hello? This is Blaine Hollis. How can I help you?"

Blaine Hollis? She didn't think that was the name she'd seen on the website. Had she dialed the wrong number? Her fingers hadn't been shaking that badly, had they?

"Oh, hello, I thought I was about to get a voicemail." Shelby's words spilled out in a frantic ramble. She took a calming breath and tried again. "My name is Shelby Doll. I'm the director of the Southlake Community Center. Perhaps you know that we serve the community as a low cost alternative for after school and summer care for children." Ugh, she sounded like a bad saleswoman, the kind who didn't know what to say and so just rattled off all the details.

"I'm calling because we are looking for donations to keep our doors open. I don't know if your organization does that sort of thing, but I wondered if there might be any players on your team who would be willing to host a clinic that we could charge for or an autograph signing or something." Shelby shook her head as she paused. She really should have scripted her speech better. Practiced it on Kenzi or something.

"You want a football player to come and host a clinic at the community center?"

The man on the other end said the words slowly and thoughtfully, but Shelby wasn't sure if he was mocking her or just chewing the idea over.

"Yes, sir. It would be great community service, and I imagine it would be a great outreach for the team as well. Meet the community, sign some autographs, I'm sure your fans would eat it up." Finally, she sounded like someone who knew what she was talking about. She waited as the silence drew out. What was he thinking?

"What did you say your name was again?"

"Shelby. Shelby Doll."

"Well, Shelby Doll, I think I know of just the player for you."

She could hear the smile in his voice and her heart sped up. Could she really be about to get her miracle? "You do?"

"I do. His name is Tucker Jackson. I'll send him over this afternoon and you can work out the details."

Shelby felt like jumping from her chair and dancing around the room. "Thank you. Thank you so much."

"No, thank you, Shelby."

She found his wording odd as she hung up the phone. Why did he sound as if she had just given him the miracle instead of the other way around?

"They have someone?" Kenzi asked.

She had been so quiet that Shelby had forgotten she was still in the room. "Yeah, a Tucker Jackson."

Kenzi's eyes grew to quarters as her head dropped forward, sending her brown hair swishing across her thin shoulders. "Tucker Jackson? The running back?"

"Uh, maybe?" Shelby wasn't even sure what a running back was much less if Tucker Jackson was one. "I didn't ask. The guy said he'd be here this afternoon."

"Oh my gosh. This is huge. Can I take a slightly longer lunch to go home and change?"

"Change?" Shelby's eyes roamed over Kenzi's outfit. Tight stretchy pants that accentuated her figure and a flowy blouse was her outfit of choice today. Not exactly what Shelby would classify as professional attire, but Kenzi generally worked with the kids where her full outfit was rarely seen by parents, and no one had complained yet. "Why? You look fine."

"Yes, but fine is what you wear when the cute UPS guy is stopping by with a package. It is not what you wear when Tucker Jackson, star running back for the Texas Tornadoes, is stopping by." Kenzi flashed her best puppy dog face and clasped her hands together under her chin. "Please?"

"Fine." Shelby rolled her eyes. She certainly hoped Kenzi didn't lose herself over this guy. It wouldn't be the first time, but she needed her friend's head in the game if they were going to save the center.

4

"Jackson, Tony, I have the perfect solution."

Tucker looked up as Blaine re-entered the room, a giant smile on his face. He had been manning Tony's phone while Tony gave Tucker an earful about public image. As if he didn't understand the importance of public image. His father had never attended a game, but he'd made sure Tucker and Whitley were by his side every time he made some big donation to the school or a local charity. "Public image," his father had told him once when he asked why they had to be there. "If the people love you, business is always better." Somehow, his father had lost sight of the fact that your children loving you was just as important.

"What solution, Blaine?" Tony's voice held a note of irritation. No doubt he'd had at least another ten minutes of brimstone he'd wanted to rail down on Tucker's head. The man was great at his job, slick and professional without being slimy; but Tucker believed he was as good as he was because he loved the sound of his own voice. He would talk your ear off any chance he got.

"I just took a call from the community center. They are looking for a way to increase revenue, and they want a football player to host a clinic and sign some autographs."

"A clinic? What would I do at a clinic?" Tucker asked. He'd heard of clinics but not usually by active players. They were normally put on by retired players looking to stay active in the limelight either to help with endorsements or because they just couldn't handle no longer being in the public eye.

Blaine shrugged. "Who cares? Teach them how to hold the ball, how to run routes, bore them with football stories, whatever you want."

"I don't think that's a good idea-"

But Tucker didn't get to finish because Tony held up his hand to interrupt him. "Now, hold on, Tucker. Blaine might be onto something. If we do this correctly, we could show you doing a good deed for the community. Build morale for both you and the team."

"But I've never held a clinic before. I wouldn't even know what to do."

"Nonsense, how hard can it be to teach a few kids how to hold the ball and run a play?" Tony asked.

Tucker shook his head. Tony had never played football, so he didn't understand the complexity behind the game. And he didn't seem like the type to hang around kids, much less teach them, but Tucker knew he wasn't going to win this argument. Besides, as far as community service, he could probably have been assigned worse. Picking up trash on the side of the road or helping out in a nursing home definitely sounded like more work than teaching kids about football.

"Will the clinic satisfy all my required hours?"

"Probably not. The team wants you to fulfill twenty hours. The clinic itself would only be a few hours, but I bet the center could use some help during the week, especially with kids being out of school for Christmas break. They are out next week, aren't they?"

Tucker shrugged. He didn't have kids, so keeping up with a school schedule was not something he did.

"Well, you can find out for sure from Shelby. If you helped out before and after practice all next week, then it might satisfy the hours. Right, Tony?" Blaine turned his attention to the PR director who was nodding thoughtfully.

"Yes, I think that could work. Try to get the clinic scheduled in the evening so parents can come. That way it benefits the kids and our fan base."

"Exactly. Plus it would show your good will and all," Blaine said.

Though he phrased it as a suggestion, Tucker knew it wasn't one. Blaine expected him to spend the next week at the center as if it were a job. "Fine, I'll report there Monday morning."

"Actually, the director is expecting you this afternoon to hash out the details of the clinic. She'll need time to organize and promote it, so you should head over there now."

Tucker sighed as he nodded. There was no use arguing with Blaine once he grabbed hold of an idea. And how hard could it be, really?

Shelby tapped her watch again and sighed. Kenzi had been gone over an hour, and their doors would open for kids in less than forty minutes. There was no way she could run the center and watch the kids by herself.

"Excuse me, I'm looking for Shelby Doll. Do you know where I can find her?"

Shelby glanced up at the masculine voice she did not recognize and blinked. A dark-haired man stood before her. His hands were shoved in the pockets of his leather jacket, and his chocolate brown eyes looked as if they'd rather be anywhere else. Normally, she might take offense to that, but at this moment, she'd rather be somewhere else too. Somewhere where she wasn't in charge, where kids weren't counting on her, and where she wouldn't have to stare at disappointed faces all day.

"I'm Shelby Doll. What can I do for you?"

"I'm Tucker Jackson. I'm the football player who will be running the clinic and whatever else you need next week."

So this was Tucker Jackson. He was definitely not what she'd expected. She'd expected someone with a friendly attitude or a smile at the very least. This man before her looked as if just being here pained him, and she wondered if he'd been assigned to do this for some reason instead of volunteering out of the goodness of his heart. She supposed she shouldn't care. Though she had no idea who he was, it was clear Kenzi did, which meant other football fans probably would as well. And she was desperate, so as long as he could be nice and bring in a crowd, he would do in her book.

She stood and extended a hand, plastering a big smile on her face in hopes it would prompt him to do the same. "Of course, Tucker. Nice to meet you. Have you ever put on a clinic before?"

"Afraid not," he said with a shake of his head and a nonchalant shrug, "but how hard can it be, right?"

Shelby swallowed her sigh. She had been hoping he would come with ideas at least, something she could work with, but it appeared she'd have to be helping him with the whole thing as well as dealing with his surly attitude.

"Okay, well, why don't you come around here and join me? We can hammer out some details." She motioned for him to proceed through the main door and then met him in the hallway.

A clean, masculine scent flooded her nose as he sat across from her, and Shelby forced herself not to focus on how handsome he was. His dark eyes were even more alluring up close as there appeared to be swirls of gold and green in them, and his jawline could have been chiseled from stone it was so perfect. If only she could wipe the expression that resembled a grimace from his face.

"So, tell me how these clinic things usually work," he said.

"Well, we open for kids at two in the afternoon during school. They are out next week for break, so we'll be open all day, but I would suggest we shoot for something around five or six as I'm sure some parents will want to get autographs from you as well. We could start a sign up today and get the word out to the local stations. Do you think Wednesday evening would give you enough time to prepare?"

Tucker paused as if running through his schedule in his head. "I have practice every afternoon next week. It usually ends by four though, so yeah, Wednesday should be fine."

She wished he sounded more excited about it. It would do her no good to have a celebrity if the celebrity acted like he'd rather be watching paint dry. "I'm sorry. I asked for someone who might draw in a crowd, and no offense, but you seem like you might push them away right now. Why exactly did they send you?"

His jaw tightened, and a tiny vein bulged in his neck. She'd obviously hit a nerve with her question. "To be honest, they sent me because I need to fulfill some community hours. Don't worry though, I'm a good actor, and I'll put on my best performance during the clinic."

"Right." His words did nothing to reassure her, but what other option did she have? He was what they had sent, and she had no time to try and find someone else. The end of the month was quickly approaching as was Christmas, so if she wanted to pay the rent and possibly provide a party for the kids, she would just have to do her best with him. "Let's do the clinic at six then, so people have time to get off work. We can offer some food for sale here so they have no excuse of missing dinner, and then you can sign autographs after. That way people have to register for the clinic to get the autographs."

"What's the money for anyway?" Tucker asked.

Shelby couldn't imagine that he really cared, but she humored the question anyway. Perhaps if he knew how important this clinic was, he could find a positive attitude. "Keeping the center open. We have a flat fee for facility use each month and a fee for the after school program, but we lost a lot of our kids when the trampoline park opened down the street, so money is tight right now, and we usually have a Christmas party for the kids. Some of them can't afford much in the way of gifts, so we try to have something small to hand out to them."

Tucker nodded as if he understood though Shelby wondered if he'd ever spent a Christmas poor. Had he ever celebrated without a tree because his family couldn't afford one? Or given coupons as gifts because there was no money to purchase anything? She doubted it, but even as the thoughts circled in her head, God convicted her. She didn't know him, didn't know his story. Maybe he had known hard times. Maybe his gruff expression had more to do with him not knowing how to run a clinic than with him not wanting to be here.

"Oh, I see our guest has arrived," Kenzi said appearing behind Tucker and mouthing, "oh my good- ness, he's dreamy" at Shelby. She had changed out of her flowy blouse and into something slightly more low-cut than Shelby preferred she wear at the center. She would have to have a talk with Kenzi about image and how her first priority had to be the kids and not Tucker.

"Hi, I'm Kenzi Lanham, Shelby's assistant." She stuck out her hand, shifting into her fake pageant queen, cheer- leader persona. It was one she had perfected, one that got her almost anything she wanted, and one that drove Shelby crazy. Shelby rolled her eyes. Kenzi didn't look as though she'd spent an hour on her face even though

Shelby knew full well that she had, and while she was glad to see her arrive before the kids did, she certainly didn't need her distracting Tucker while they tried to plan.

"Uh, Tucker Jackson, nice to meet you."

Shelby didn't miss how his eyes brightened a little when he touched Kenzi's hand. He certainly hadn't had that light in his eyes when he shook her hand, but Shelby was used to this. Kenzi had always been the outgoing one, and with her dark hair and green eyes, she was beautiful. It was no mystery that men were drawn to her. The only surprising thing was that she was still single.

Actually that part wasn't a surprise either. Kenzi had always been a little flighty. She'd dropped out of college because she didn't know what she wanted to do with her life, and she jumped from one man to another because she had no idea what she wanted in a man. However, she'd made it her mission to date as many as possible until she figured it out.

"Kenzi, Tucker and I need to plan the clinic for next week. Do you think you could make sure everything is ready for the kids who will be arriving soon?" Shelby made sure to emphasize the words so that Kenzi would realize her words weren't a question.

Kenzi's lips pursed in a slight pout as if she were going to argue, but Shelby shot her a warning glance. She was still in charge here.

"Yes, of course. Tucker, if you need anything, you can

holler for me. It was great meeting you, and I'm sure I'll see you around."

Sugar dripped from Kenzi's voice accompanied with just the right amount of eye batting. Were those false lashes? Shelby rolled her eyes. Kenzi could teach a class in flirting.

"I'm sure you will," Tucker said with a smile. "Does she work here every day?" he asked when Kenzi was out of sight. He might have been talking to Shelby, but his gaze remained at the doorway as if willing Kenzi to reappear.

"Yep, every day," Shelby said through clenched teeth. She resisted the urge to smack him to bring him back to the discussion at hand. If she had any other option, she would kick this guy to the curb. But she didn't. It was him or nothing, and nothing wasn't really an option. Not if she wanted to keep the lights on and the doors open. "I think we're almost finished here, but do you need anything else for the clinic? Any supplies?"

"What?" He blinked and then returned his gaze to her.

"Supplies. For the clinic." Perhaps if she said the words slowly and deliberately, they would register in his neanderthal head. "Do you need anything?"

"Uh, footballs, I guess, and maybe cones to set up boundaries." His face muscles twitched, and she could tell he was trying not to cave in to the desire to check the doorway again. Kenzi was pretty. Okay, more than pretty, but why did every man have to go gaga when they saw her?

"I know we have cones, and I think we have about ten footballs." She'd have to air them up the night before to make sure they weren't flat, but that wasn't a huge deal. "Will that be enough?"

"It should be fine, yeah."

"Okay, well, then I think we're good."

"Right. Uh, what about next week? What time do you want me here?"

Shelby stared at him. He hadn't even wanted to be here, but suddenly with the appearance of Kenzi, he seemed to find that appealing. She leaned back and crossed her arms. She needed him for the clinic, but she had no use for him for the rest of the week. Well, actually she did. Volunteers were hard to come by, and with the school kids out for the next two weeks, she could use another adult around. Tucker, however, seemed like he would be more interested in ogling Kenzi than helping out with the kids.

"Look," he said with a sigh, "I'm sorry. I'm no good at this. This whole situation wasn't my fault, and I guess I'm a little irritated that it feels like I'm being punished for it."

She had no idea what situation he was even talking about. The clinic? Or whatever he had done that had resulted in him being volunteered to run the clinic?

"My team wants me to fulfill twenty hours of community service, and they expect me to serve it here. Helping out. So, what can I do?"

Shelby regarded him a moment longer. She wanted to tell him no, that she didn't need his scowling face around the center, but her conscience told her that maybe he had been given a raw deal. Being punished for something she hadn't done would probably make her angry, and perhaps she would have a similar reaction if she were thrown into unknown territory like he clearly was. Besides, it was Christmas, and she could use the help.

"Fine. We aren't open on the weekend, but next week, we're open all day because there's no school. If you can be here at eight am, I can put you to work."

He blanched slightly and blinked at her as if shocked by the time. For a moment, Shelby thought he was going to retract his offer, but then he squared his broad shoulders and nodded. "I'll have to leave in the middle of the day for practice, but I can come by before and return after if you need as well."

"Sounds good. The kids will be here soon. You're welcome to stay and meet them if you'd like, and if you want a tour of the center, I'm sure Kenzi would be glad to show you around." She didn't know why she was offering, but maybe she hoped he would get Kenzi out of his system before next week.

"I might just do that," he said, "Thanks." And before

she could say another word, he had ducked out of the room.

"You're welcome," she said sarcastically to the now-empty chair. Shelby knew it wasn't Kenzi's fault, and she had no desire to date someone like Tucker Jackson; but she did wonder why she couldn't get him out of her head. He was not her type, nor did he seem to want to be here; but still she found his face popping into her mind. His dark eyes, his strong jaw, his broad shoulders. Why? With a sigh, she shook her head. That worry could wait for another day. She had much more important things to worry about right now, like the fact that the kids would be arriving at any moment; and she needed to be prepared.

$$ \text{❧} \quad 5 \quad \text{❧} $$

Tucker crossed the big gym and glanced around for Kenzi. He didn't see her in the main room, but there were a few doorways leading out of the room. Perhaps she was down one of them. As he headed toward the first doorway, his gaze travelled the faded white walls. The building could definitely use a little TLC. Not only did faded paint cover the walls, but scratches marred the floor. More than that though was the ambiance. The place felt sad, like happiness had packed up its bags and left. Tucker shivered and wondered why kids came here at all. Was there really no other place they could afford?

He couldn't imagine having to spend time in a place like this; but then again, he'd never had to. Before his mother had died, he'd had her to go home to; and after that, his father's money had paid for sports teams and leagues to keep him busy after school. What did these kids have going for them? Well, they had Shelby and Kenzi. They both seemed nice enough. Maybe they brightened the place up.

Tucker found Kenzi hauling a rack of sports equipment out of a supply closet. She was certainly a perk he hadn't expected. When Blaine had said a woman ran the center, Tucker had hoped perhaps she might be easy on the eyes; but while Shelby was pretty, she was also the epitome of uptight. Her hair had been meticulously sprayed into place in a tight bun - all but one tendril that had somehow snuck loose - and she dressed more like an old time librarian than a manager in her pencil skirt and button-down shirt. There was something about her though, something that sparked when they shook hands. Kenzi, on the other hand, was bright and cheery and definitely more concerned with her appearance than her boss.

"Can I help with that?" He flashed his most disarming smile at her and was pleased when she returned it in kind.

"Sure, thanks. Did you get everything settled with Shelby?"

"I think so. I'll have to spend some time this weekend figuring out exactly what I'm teaching these kids, but it should be fine."

She tilted her head coyly at him. "Somehow, I don't think you'll have any problem coming up with something."

"Thanks." He stared at her for a moment before asking the question that had been burning on his mind since the moment he saw her. "I have to ask. What are you doing working in a place like this? It doesn't really seem to suit your," he paused, trying to think of the appropriate word, "style, at least not like it does Shelby."

"No, I'm definitely not like Shelby," Kenzi said with a laugh. Her gaze traveled to the reception area, "but she's my best friend and she has a heart of gold. When she needed someone to help out at the center, I stepped up, partly to see her in action and partly because I think I'm hoping some of her rubs off on me."

She wanted to be more like Shelby? "Why?" He hadn't meant to say the question aloud, but it had slipped out.

Kenzi focused her green eyes on him. "Because she's the best person I know. I grew up with money and had anything I wanted, but Shelby?" She shook her head. "Shelby worked for everything she has. She began volunteering in this center when she was in high school because she felt called to. Then she worked here part time while she attended college. She could be managing any place she wanted, she's that amazing; but she chose to come back here. To give back to her community. I only hope that one day I'm as selfless as she is."

Tucker looked back toward the reception area with new eyes. Perhaps he'd been too hard on Shelby. What was it Blaine had said? That he needed to see how the less fortunate lived? Maybe Blaine hadn't been as privileged as Tucker thought. Maybe he was someone like Shelby, who'd known hard times and come out better on the other side because of them. Guilt the size of Texas settled on Tucker's shoulders. He'd been throwing himself a grand pity party over having to do a little community service while Shelby willingly gave of herself to help those around her.

"You sure were talking to Tucker for quite a while." Shelby flashed Kenzi a look out of the corner of her eye as she shut down the computer for the night. Tucker had stayed for an hour talking with Kenzi after he finished with Shelby, but at least he had been nice to the kids. Or she figured he had because no one had complained.

Kenzi shrugged. "I guess. We mainly talked about you though."

"Me?" Shelby nearly choked on the word. "Why would you talk about me? What did you say?"

Kenzi rolled her eyes. "Relax. I simply told him how amazing you were and how you give your all for these kids."

Kenzi never ceased to amaze Shelby. One minute, she was leaving Shelby hanging by taking an extended lunch break to doll up for some guy, and the next, she was singing her praises to the very same man. "Well, thanks, but I doubt he cares about stuff like that. He said he was here because the team assigned him community service. I think he'd rather be anywhere else, and if I had any other way to bring money in, I might just let him go." She grabbed her coat and purse and flicked off the lights.

"Don't be too hard on him," Kenzi said. "I get the feeling he's a good guy underneath. He just hasn't figured out how to show it yet."

"Hmph. I hope he figures it out by Monday, or his surly attitude might send the last few clients we have running for the hills."

Kenzi linked her arm through Shelby's as they walked toward the front door. "First of all, he was great with the kids. I saw no surly attitude, but second, what is it you always tell me about worrying?"

"That you don't do it enough?" Shelby asked.

"No. That you can't change tomorrow by worrying about it. God's got this. Right?"

Shelby paused and stared at her friend. She had always said that. At least until she became the manager, and her worry load tripled. Perhaps it was time to take her own advice and turn those worries over to God. Heaven knew she hadn't been doing a great job trying to take care of things on her own. Perhaps, this was God's way of showing her that. "You're right. God's got this, and He will provide one way or another."

Kenzi's face broke into a wide smile. "That's my girl. Now, how about we grab dinner out somewhere? It's so late that I'm sure you've missed the family dinner."

Shelby glanced at her watch. Kenzi was right. Her mother always served dinner promptly at seven, so no one could use the excuse that they didn't know what time it might be. Normally, Shelby was closed up by six forty five and, thanks to the close proximity of the center to her parent's house, managed to pull into the driveway ten minutes later, but tonight closing had run long. It was already past seven thirty, and her stomach groaned in protest at the extra wait time.

"Okay, what do you have in mind?"

"Just a little Thai place I've been meaning to try for ages. We'll take my car, and I'll bring you back here for yours later. Deal?" Kenzi wiggled her eyebrows the way she had in college when she wanted to get Shelby to lighten up and give up studying for the night. It was a comical effect on her flawless face but one that always managed to elicit a smile from Shelby.

Shelby rolled her eyes; but just like in college, she couldn't keep her mouth from twitching into a smile. She locked the front door and then faced Kenzi. "Fine. Deal."

"Yes. We're going to have so much fun."

Shelby wasn't sure about that, but as she followed Kenzi to her car, she couldn't deny that she felt a little lighter. Like maybe everything would turn out all right.

❦ 6 ❦

Tucker groaned as the blaring beeping blasted away his peaceful slumber. He hated alarm clocks. It was just one of the many reasons he enjoyed the football lifestyle. Since practices rarely started before noon, he almost never had to wake up to the harsh sound of the alarm. Instead, he could lie in bed and wake up leisurely with the sun. At least, normally he could. Today, he had to be out of the house in an hour. He'd told Shelby he would be there when the center opened, and that was less than two hours from now.

He drug himself out of bed and plodded toward the shower. It was still dark outside and cold, so cold. Perhaps he should look into those heated floors after all. Most of the house was carpeted, but the bathroom had cold marble flooring. Easy to clean but like an ice box when it was cold.

Tucker stepped into the shower and turned the water to hot. He'd always enjoyed the steam, but it was even more invigorating today. It pushed the last bit of sleep from his eyes, but it also had the unfortunate effect of clearing the fog from his head which allowed his mind to think about the day ahead. What in the world would he do with kids all day? They had seemed nice Friday evening, but he had only spent an hour there. Most of that had been introducing himself and then talking with Kenzi while they kept an eye on the kids. Today would be longer, and he wasn't much of a kid person. Maybe that was due to the fact that he'd had to grow up so quickly. Maybe it was the reminder of his own past before his mother died. Whatever the reason, he'd never been great with kids. Sure, he would sign their footballs and shirts and pose for pictures, but he was always glad when the kids were gone from the crowd.

With a sigh, he turned the water off and stepped out of the shower. He would just have to make the best of the situation. After all, it was only for a week. One week, and then his service would be over. He could concentrate on the game and return to sleeping in.

Shelby glanced up from the flyer she was making as the door opened. Tucker Jackson strode through right on time. She'd had her doubts that he would show up again, but she supposed she was glad. Her high school volunteer who normally helped out during Christmas Break had texted her last night stating she didn't feel well and probably wouldn't make it in for the day, which would have left Kenzi and Shelby in quite a pickle if Tucker hadn't shown up. Though their count was low enough that two people could watch the kids, it would mean no break for either of them all day, and that made for a long day. Hopefully, Jennifer's illness was temporary and not typical high school flaking. She had seemed responsible, but Shelby had noticed a shift in the younger generation.

"Perfect timing," she said as he signed in on the log. "Can you come around here? I need to have you fill out a volunteer form, and I'd like to see what you think of this flyer for your clinic." She'd mentioned the event to the parents when they picked up their kids on Friday, but she wanted flyers to give the kids to take home as a reminder and to hand out to anyone new. Plus, she hoped to find some time to post a few around the town today.

"Uh, sure." He might have been speaking to her, but she thought that his eyes were definitely looking for Kenzi. Shelby tried not to let it bother her. After all, she was used to being in Kenzi's shadow, but she couldn't deny that a part of her wanted to step out, to be noticed for once.

He appeared in the doorway a moment later, and she waved him into the room. She slid the volunteer form she had pulled earlier across the table to him.

"What's this?" he asked as he picked up the paper.

"The volunteer form. Every volunteer has to fill one out. I should have had you do it the last time you were here, but I forgot. It's straightforward information - name, address, phone number, blood type."

His eyes shot up. "Blood type?"

Shelby bit back her smile; she hadn't thought he would be this easy to tease. She put on her best serious face and tried to keep her voice neutral. "Of course, just in case you fall or the kids attack you and we need to rush you to the hospital."

He cocked his head at her and narrowed his eyes. "You're joking with me, aren't you?"

"Yes, I am." Shelby forced her face to remain deadpan though she could feel the giggle building inside her. "We haven't had anyone fall around here in a very long time."

He shook his head and began filling out the form, and Shelby counted the seconds in her head. How long would it take him to realize-

His head shot up. "Wait, the kids don't really attack people, do they?"

The giggle escaped her lips at the slight panic in his eyes. He was way too gullible. "No, I'm kidding. It's really just so we can get ahold of you if necessary, and we have to keep a record in case anything ever happens that needs to be investigated. Don't worry, though, it never has."

"I didn't take you for having such a sense of humor," Tucker said as a small smile pulled at his own lips.

Sense of humor. Yep. That's what she had. Kenzi had the magnetic smile, personality, and figure; and Shelby had... Humor. "There's a lot you don't know about me," she said softly under her breath. She didn't think she'd said it loud enough for him to hear, but when he paused and glanced at her from the corner of his eye, she had to wonder. Thankfully, he said nothing though, just continued filling out the form.

"Okay, all done." He clicked the back of the pen before laying it on the paper and sliding both her direction.

"Thanks." She picked up the form and rolled back to the desk, placing it in a manilla file folder next to her computer.

"There's already a file on me?" he asked.

"What?" She chuckled and shook her head as he grinned at her. So, he had a sense of humor too. "Yeah, the team sent over your rap sheet. I had no idea." She'd meant the words as a joke, but as his jaw tightened, she could tell that something had hit too close to home. *Did* he have a rap sheet? Was that why he had been assigned community service? He hadn't actually told her what he'd done. Had he done something worth being punished for?

He'd said it hadn't been his fault, but had he been lying? She wanted to know more, but she could tell he wasn't going to open up about it. Surely, it couldn't be anything that bad. They wouldn't send someone violent to a center to work with kids, would they? No, of course they wouldn't; she was just being paranoid.

"Um, well anyway, here's the flyer I've been working on for the clinic. Can you tell me what you think?" He crossed the small room to stand beside her, and the scent of his woodsy cologne filled her nose. He wasn't as tall as her brothers, but there was something solid and masculine about his presence. A tremor raced down her back, and she forced herself not to shiver.

"It looks good," he said, "but you might want to include the price. People won't like it if they think it's free and then we charge them when they show up. How much are you charging anyway?"

"I'm not sure. I know you haven't done this before, but what do you think is a good rate? Fifty dollars? More? Less?" She'd crunched a few numbers over the weekend and knew they needed to charge as much as people would be willing to pay, but she wanted to hear his thoughts too.

He ran his hand across his jaw. The soft scratch of skin against stubble filled the silence. "I think fifty is too low. Plus, you're trying to increase enrollment, right?"

Shelby nodded. "That is the ultimate goal. I need to pay January's rent first and foremost, but getting more kids back in the program is the only way we'll succeed long term."

He pursed his lips as if thinking again. "I know you want all your kids to be able to attend, but what if we have a sliding scale? The price is one hundred per kid, fifty for those who are current members, and seventy-five for anyone who signs up for the next month and pays in advance. Plus, you could offer a discount for families who have more than one kid."

Shelby blinked, blindsided by his logic. She hadn't known many athletes in high school, preferring to hang around students who read or debated instead; but she'd had a generalization in her head about them. Stereotypical jocks who only thought about how to bulk up, win, and get girls. Tucker was proving that wrong. "That's a great idea. How do you seem to know so much about charging rates? I thought you said you'd never done this before."

His smile faltered, and a small sigh proceeded his words. "My father is a prolific donor. I'm pretty sure he could turn it into an Olympic event if he wanted. Needless to say, I've heard all the spiels, read all the flyers, and deciphered all the doublespeak."

She nodded and began typing in the corrections. There was obviously a story here between him and his father, but again Shelby didn't pry. She was great at listening, but he didn't know her well enough to open up to her;

and whatever was going on between them had affected him greatly. It probably still was.

"Better?" she asked when she finished.

He leaned over her shoulder again and nodded. "Yeah, now it looks great."

"Good, thank you. Did you think of anything else you might need?" She turned to look at him and nearly jumped out of her skin at how close his face was. Her heart thundered in her chest.

"No, I think I'm good." His eyes held hers a moment before he leaned back. "What would you like me to do today?"

"Um." Shelby was still trying to get her heart under control. Why was she reacting like this around him? He wasn't interested in her; he'd made it abundantly clear that he preferred Kenzi. So, why did she feel like a giddy schoolgirl? "The kids will be arriving soon. Do you want to air up the balls and make sure they're ready to go?"

"I'd be happy to. Where do I find them?"

Shelby grabbed the supply room key from the rack and then handed it to him. She walked to the doorway and pointed to the far side of the large gym wall. "Straight over there. You can't miss it."

He tossed her a lopsided smile as he walked away, and Shelby took a deep breath. She needed to get herself under control. Tucker was volunteering. Nothing more. And she would do well to remember that.

Tucker forced himself not to glance back at Shelby as he walked toward the supply closet. What had happened in there? Yes, it had been nice to see her sense of humor, but she was so not his type. So, what had that moment been about? That moment where they locked eyes and he felt like she was glimpsing his soul? It must just be the situation. He was out of his element here. His guard had just been down. That was all. Right?

He opened the supply closet and flicked the light on. The room was tiny, barely larger than a single stall bathroom. One silver rack filled with basketballs, footballs, and volleyballs took up most of the space. Though the rack was full, all of the balls appeared to be low on air. He wondered if they had ever been filled up before, but as he inspected them closer, he realized that wasn't the issue. These balls were old and worn. He looked around for an air pump and spied an older hand held model in the back corner. It too appeared to have seen better days. He surveyed the rest of the supplies with fresh eyes and realized everything in the center could stand to be replaced. It was a wonder Shelby was keeping this place open at all.

He grabbed the air pump in one hand and the silver rack in the other and wheeled it out to the main area. The basketballs were on top, so he started with them. He had just inserted the needle when he heard high-heeled steps behind him.

"Hey, Tucker, Shelby said you were airing up the balls. Would you like some help?"

Kenzi wore tight jeans that showed off her toned legs and an oversized sweater today. Her smile was just as bright as it had been on Friday, and he felt himself mirroring her expression. "I'd love that, but there appears to only be one pump." Her face fell in disappointment, and he hurriedly continued, "But, you could hold the needle in while I pump, and it might go faster."

"Sure, I can do that." She picked up the ball and cradled it in one arm while holding the needle in place with her other hand. Not the way he would have done it, but he supposed it worked.

"So, I know you said you started working here to help Shelby out, but how long has it been?" he asked as he began pumping the handle.

"Only for the past year since Shelby became the director. I went to college for a time, but I didn't really know what I wanted to do, so I'm taking time off while I decide. I volunteered a few times with Shelby before she took over and enjoyed it; so when she offered me a full-time position, it seemed like a good job until I figure out where I want to go."

He took the ball from her and squeezed. It felt full enough, so he removed the needle and bounced it. Satisfied, he placed it back in the rack and handed her the next one. "So, you still don't know what you want to do?"

She shrugged. "Not really. I like talking to people and I'd love anything where I could be in the public eye, like a reporter or something, but I don't want to jump into anything until I'm really sure. So, for now, I work with Shelby. It pays the bills and allows me to meet people."

Tucker couldn't imagine not knowing what he wanted to do with his life at this age. From the time he'd started playing football his freshman year of high school, he'd known that was what he wanted to do. But he supposed it happened. He'd attended college with several people who floated from one major to the next because they couldn't decide what career path they wanted.

Still, it was odd how different Shelby and Kenzi were. He'd thought it was just the outside appearance, but it evidently ran deeper. Shelby not only appeared more professional in her attire, but she also seemed to know what she wanted out of life. Whereas Kenzi screamed fun with her tighter, brighter clothing, but he wondered how long the fun would last. He wasn't sure he was ready to settle down; but when he was, he wanted someone who knew where they were going.

"Have you always played football?"

Kenzi's voice shook him back to the present. She had shelved the second ball and was inserting the needle into the third. "Um, since high school. I began playing my freshman year, and not only did it turn out I was pretty good at it, but it was an escape for me."

"An escape?" Tiny wrinkles crossed her forehead as she scrunched her brow. "What did you need to escape from?"

Tucker opened his mouth to answer, but he wasn't sure he was ready to talk about his mother's death. Nor was he sure he wanted to tell Kenzi. He didn't know why, but he sensed Shelby would understand his pain more than Kenzi would. "Oh, you know, high school angst and all that," he said instead. "Do you have high schoolers who come here?" He couldn't imagine a high school student enjoying time in the center. It was too plain, too outdated.

"No, most of our kids are elementary and middle school aged."

"That makes sense. I suppose once you can drive, you can take care of yourself." Or once your mother dies and your father withdraws, he thought to himself.

"Yeah, it's too bad more don't volunteer though. We have one girl, Jennifer, who helps out during breaks and summers, but we could use more. I think teenagers could be great mentors for the younger students, but I remember high school. The last thing I wanted to do was give up my time after school, especially to hang out with younger kids." She placed the third and last basketball on the shelf and turned to the footballs.

Tucker eyed the faded and worn pigskin as she

inserted the needle. "Are those all the footballs the center has?"

"Yeah, Shelby has been wanting to replace them forever, but she hasn't had the money. Most of what we make pays rent and our salaries. She pays a part time janitor, but his job is next on the chopping block, so replacement equipment just keeps dropping lower on the list."

Tucker glanced back at the office where he was sure Shelby sat trying to figure out a way to bring in more money. A sting of something he didn't recognize tugged at his heart. Pity? No, that wasn't quite it. Sorrow? He couldn't even give it a name. All he knew was that he felt for Shelby. She was trying so hard to keep the center open, and she certainly wasn't doing it for money or fame like most people he knew. In fact, the thought convicted him. Maybe he could do something more to help out. More than just the clinic and volunteering this week.

※ 7 ※

Tucker pulled into the stadium parking lot and took a deep breath as he turned off the engine. He couldn't believe how tired he was already. Unsure if it was due to the early morning or the hours spent with the kids, he feared he would be dragging during practice today. And he didn't think he could afford to do that. A frustrated sigh escaped his lips as he grabbed his bag of gear off the passenger seat and headed toward the locker room. He would have to push the exhaustion away and make sure his focus was on practice.

Practices were normally his favorite time of the day, but now? Not only was he tired, but anxiety gnawed at the back of his brain. It was his first practice since the incident last Thursday, and he didn't know what to expect. Had

Blaine told everyone else about the assault? Had they found out by some other means? Would they treat him differently? It had already been a struggle trying to fit in on this team after the trade. He certainly didn't need anything else alienating him.

Tucker glanced at his watch again. He was half an hour early, but he'd planned it that way to make sure he was dressed and ready before anyone else. Now that he had a blemish on his record, he would have to toe the line from here on out or start adding some positive checks to his name to clear the stigma. What better way than to be prepared for practice? He'd had to leave the center a little earlier than he'd planned, but he'd promised Shelby he would return after practice.

He pulled open the heavy metal door that squeaked loud enough to wake the dead. Someone should really put some oil on it. Perhaps he should add that to his list as a good deed. As he turned the corner to the locker area, he stopped short. He hadn't expected to see anyone here yet, but there was Blaine, already dressed in his practice jersey and reading a book as he leaned against his locker. Tucker hadn't really pegged Blaine as a big reader.

"You get everything ironed out with the center?" Blaine asked as Tucker dropped his bag on the bench that sat in between the two rows of lockers.

"Yeah, the clinic is scheduled for Wednesday night at

six, so I may have to leave practice early." Tucker opened his locker and took out his helmet, setting it next to his bag before unzipping the large duffel and pulling his practice gear out.

"That's no problem. We'll probably be done earlier that night anyway. You're going there this evening after practice right?"

Tucker wasn't sure if Blaine was asking out of curiosity or to check up on him and make sure he was filling his part of the bargain, but he guessed the latter. "Yes, I'm going there tonight, and I was there this morning."

"Good. Don't forget. Every day this week. The director will be keeping track for me. You definitely don't want to miss a day or you might find yourself missing the next game." He placed a bookmark in his book, closed it, and shoved it in his locker. "I'll see you out on the field."

And then he was gone, and Tucker was alone in the locker room. With a sigh, he peeled off his shirt and changed into his practice one. He hated having to answer to Blaine. The man appeared too perfect, and Tucker wondered if he ever did anything wrong. He would definitely be relieved when this week ended.

Shelby stared at the list of possible donors she had created and sighed. Calling businesses and asking for money was not her strong suit, but it had to be done. Her calculations showed that even if all the current kids and the ones who had left attended the clinic they would have enough for another month of rent, maybe two, but that was it. And that was if all the kids attended which Shelby knew was not a reality. Some would be busy, some wouldn't be able to afford it, and some might not even care about football. That meant she needed to get the word out to the community and quickly. Her hope was that by calling the local businesses, she might be able to drop off flyers tonight or tomorrow morning for them to hang up; and if she was really lucky, she might be able to secure a few donations in exchange for sponsorship mentions.

Her first call though had to be to the newspaper and radio stations. It was short notice, but she hoped they would be able to run a PSA or something. She had tried to call on Friday, but by the time she'd had everything hammered out with Tucker, no one had been answering the phones.

"Woodville Gazette, how may I direct your call?" the woman on the other end said.

"Hello, this is Shelby Doll from the community center. I'm not sure who I need, but I was hoping to speak with someone about running an ad for an event we have coming up on Wednesday."

"That would be Marcia Walker. I'll connect you."

Shelby held her breath as the phone rang and rang and rang. She sighed when the voicemail picked up. She had been hoping to talk to a real person; but as time was of the essence, a voicemail would have to do. Hopefully, Marcia would call back, but if not, she'd try again tomorrow morning. She left a voice message and then replaced the phone in the cradle.

The next number yielded a voicemail as well. As did the place after that. By the time she finished the list, she had only reached two businesses. Both had agreed to let her hang flyers, but only one was considering a donation. "Holiday times are tough," they'd said which had made Shelby nearly laugh out loud. Didn't they know that was the exact reason she was calling?

She wondered when the shift had happened. When exactly had people stopped donating? She'd noticed it over the years even as a volunteer - fewer and fewer donations coming in, but this year had to be the worst. And it wasn't just the community center. She'd noticed it at church too. People had stopped putting tithes in the offering plate when it was passed. She supposed some people gave online like she did, but her church always put the count of money received each week, and she'd noticed it getting smaller and smaller.

"Hey, last kid is gone and Tucker and I straightened

up," Kenzi said knocking on the doorframe. "You gonna head out of here some time tonight?"

"Yeah, I was just trying to get us some coverage for the clinic on Wednesday, but it's not looking good. I'm going to canvas the businesses tomorrow to see about posting flyers. Did you make sure all the kids got one?"

"We did."

"I might have an idea," Tucker said, appearing behind Kenzi. "I could check with the PR rep for the Tornadoes and see if they would put something on our website."

Shelby's heart soared. "That would be amazing exposure. Do you think he'll do it?"

Tucker shrugged. "I don't see why not unless it's a time thing, but I'll call him as soon as I leave here. Was there anything else you needed?"

"Not for tonight." Shelby shut off the computer and grabbed her purse. "It's time to call it a night anyway." She pulled on her coat and flicked the light off. Maybe things would work out after all. If Tucker could get the clinic up on the webpage, that would have to draw in some new people. She followed Kenzi and Tucker toward the door, dropping her head to rummage for her keys in her purse.

"Oh my gosh, it's snowing."

"What?" Shelby's head popped up at Kenzi's statement. Sure enough, tiny flakes flitted past the window.

Snow? Why was it snowing? They lived in central Texas where it almost never snowed.

"I knew it," Tucker said as he pushed open the door. "I felt it the other night. That chill in the air."

"It can't snow." Shelby locked the front door and then pulled on her gloves. "What if it keeps people from coming to the clinic?"

"Don't worry," Kenzi said, tilting her head back and opening her mouth to catch a snowflake. "It's barely anything. I doubt it even sticks."

But Shelby wasn't so sure. The little voice of doubt in her head had started up again. What if it wasn't just a dusting? What if it turned into something more? What if it snowed enough that they had to cancel the clinic?

Unlocking her car, she climbed inside and turned the key to let the engine warm up. As she did, she watched the flakes of snow glide past her window. "Please stop snowing," she whispered as her eyes scanned the gray clouds. They were dark and heavy, and right now they were teasing her; but she knew at any moment they would open up and dump the snow they were concealing. It would blanket the ground, sending tremors of excitement through all the kids as they prayed for enough snow to build a snowman or go sledding or have a snowball fight. Daggers of disappointment would pierce all the parents as they dreaded having to drive on the icy streets.

Shelby usually loved the snow; she always had. Memo-

ries of playing in the snow with her big brothers and
building giant snowmen with her dad were some of her
favorites from when she was young. Of course, here in
Texas, it didn't snow nearly as often as it had in Nebraska
where she grew up until her father's company moved them
out to Fort Worth; but she still always prayed for snow
every December.

Her mother had never enjoyed the snow as much as
Shelby had. Perhaps she had when she was little, but snow
in Nebraska rarely closed businesses, and it almost never
closed hospitals. As her mother was a nurse, it had often
meant her getting up for work extra early to drive the
snowy streets safely. Then her shift had been full of
helping others who were not so cautious, and finally when
her shift ended, generally after running at least an hour
later than planned, she would have to make the treach-
erous drive back home in the dark. Shelby had never fully
understood why her mother didn't enjoy the snow.
Until now.

Now, as the cold from the outside invaded her car and
chilled her insides, she could understand her mother's
reaction. Now that she had responsibilities and an
upcoming event that dangled precariously already, she
could see the snow not for the magical wonderland that it
was, but for the havoc wreaking disaster it might become.

If it snowed too much, the center would have to close
which would be disastrous with the unpaid rent hanging

over her head and the Christmas party still not funded. Plus, delivering flyers and asking for donations would be a lot harder if Shelby had to do it trudging through snow. Even worse, the snow might keep people from attending the clinic. And then where would she get the money?

Though she didn't normally pray for God to influence the weather, she found herself doing it now as she drove to her parent's house. "Lord, please don't let the snow stick. Please let it pass us. You know how much this center means to the community and the kids. Please."

Shelby groaned as the snow fell heavier, and her windshield wipers worked extra hard keeping her windshield cleared. The rhythmic swishing of their blades sent her heart pounding even faster as the scene outside her window became more like a snowglobe freshly shaken.

How she used to love snow globes. They were the one trinket she always bought when her family took a trip somewhere. Sam always bought a shot glass, Scott collected hats, but Shelby had always gravitated to the snow globes. For a time, they had lined her shelves; and some nights, she would take one to bed, shake it, and wish she could live in the tiny house or village that appeared so peacefully nestled in the swirling snow. As she grew older, her interest in them had waned. She wasn't even sure where they had ended up after she moved out though, and she hadn't thought of them in ages. They were forefront in her mind now, however, as the snow grew thicker and swirled lazily out the window; and unless Shelby was imagining it, the ground sported a fresh white color in places. It was sticking.

She parked the car in her parent's driveway and rushed inside. The warmth from their heater blanketed her as she shook the white powder from her hair.

"Oh no, is it snowing?" her mother asked as she entered the room.

"It is," Shelby growled as she removed her shoes. "It started off light, but it's definitely getting thicker out there. I'm praying that it stops."

Her mother's brow lifted. "You? Praying it stops? I thought you loved the snow."

"I do, but it's the worst time right now. If it keeps snowing, it might cancel the clinic I have planned on Wednesday; and without that, I don't know how we're going to get the money we need."

"Well, I'm sure God will provide for you. Heaven knows we need the center to give those kids a safe place after school and during breaks. Try not to worry about it too much right now. Dinner's ready. Are you hungry?"

Shelby spared one more glance out the front window before heaving a resigned sigh, nodding, and following her mother to the dining room.

Scott, Sam, Iris, and her father were already seated around the large table when Shelby and her mother entered. The extra leaf had been put in, but it was still a tight squeeze for six of them. She wondered what would happen when she and Scott got married. Would her parents purchase a larger table or would the family dinners fall apart? She certainly hoped it wasn't the latter. Except for Kenzi, who could always get her to talk, these family dinners were the only other place Shelby really felt comfortable, whole, loved.

"Ah, there's my two favorite girls," her father said as they pulled out their chairs. "For a moment, I thought we were going to have to start without you."

"No, sorry, I just had to drive slower due to the snow," Shelby said as she sat in her chair.

"Is it snowing?" Iris craned her head around Sam to see out the dining room window.

"It is and getting thicker by the minute. I could use some prayer that it stops before it shuts down my fundraiser scheduled for Wednesday," Shelby said. "The center could certainly use the money."

"Well, why don't we add that to the prayer for tonight," her father said as he held out his hand. Around the table everyone grabbed the hand next to them and bowed their heads. "Lord, we thank you for this food that you have provided. We thank you for the time we are able to spend together as a family and for the jobs you have given us all. Please help the community center find funding to stay open. We know there are many in this town who are struggling and need the doors to stay open. In your name, Amen."

"Amen," Shelby echoed as she opened her eyes. She glanced out the window, but the thick snowflakes now looked more like a white curtain than individual crystals. It appeared God was not in the business of granting miracles tonight.

8

Darkness still filled the room when Shelby's alarm went off, but it took her only moments to shake the sleep from her eyes. She had to check the snow. Pushing the plush comforter back, she swung her legs out and into her fluffy leopard print house shoes that she always kept by the side of her bed. Even though her room was carpeted, it was always cold in the morning. The poor heater just couldn't seem to keep up with the draft that drifted in through the old windows.

A few steps brought her to the window, and she pulled back the curtains. The streetlight gave just enough illumination to see that snow still fell softly to the completely white ground. She let the curtain fall back over the window and padded back to her nightstand where the remote sat.

She punched the button and the old television hummed to life. It was a flat screen, but not the fancy ones that were so popular today. She had no Apple TV, no Roku device, and definitely no 3D. No, this was a television she had purchased used when her last television gave up the ghost. The screen flickered for a moment before coming into focus, and Shelby curled her feet up under her to watch the news report.

"While we expected snow, we did not predict it would happen this quickly or that we would get this much," the woman on the screen said. Her blond hair fell in perfect waves to her thin shoulders, and though Shelby had often heard that TV cameras made people look ten pounds heavier, this woman didn't appear to have any extra weight on her. Her hand motioned to the screen behind her, and Shelby marveled at how good she was at making it appear she could see the image on the screen when Shelby knew a green screen was the only thing behind the woman. It was fascinating technology.

"The streets are still slick and the DOT is recommending that you give yourself an extra half hour of driving time to navigate the icy roads. The good news is that the sun is expected to come out today and temperatures are expected to rise to the mid forties melting all the snow by late afternoon."

"Yes," Shelby jumped up from the bed and danced an awkward jig over to her closet. She might not have rhythm but what she lacked in style, she made up for in exuberance. And she knew just who to thank this morning. The snow would be gone by tomorrow which meant the clinic could continue as planned.

She jumped in the shower, whistling as she washed. Maybe they could even take the kids out back to play in the snow if they all brought warm enough coats. She knew they would go stir crazy if they were stuck in the center while the snow taunted them from the ground.

Her joy lasted through breakfast, through brushing her teeth, and bundling up for the cold. It even lasted through the slightly terrifying drive where she almost swerved off the road when she was forced to brake at the bottom of a slight hill, but it died as she pulled into the parking lot of the community center. She had no idea why, but an ominous feeling that something was wrong fell on her shoulders as she parked the car and got out.

Nothing looked out of place. Snow covered the roof, but thankfully, it still looked to be in one piece. The windows weren't cracked or broken, so what was it?

With careful, deliberate steps, she made her way up the sidewalk. She'd have to get some salt on it quickly before anyone slipped and fell. Hopefully they had some in the supply shed. The supply shed? Had something happened to it? Was that why she felt something was wrong? She quickly veered to the right and toward the shed, but when she rounded the corner, she stopped. The shed looked fine, and the lock still hung securely on the door. So, that wasn't it either.

Shaking her head, she returned to the center and unlocked the front door. The lights flicked on like normal, so it wasn't the loss of electricity that bothered her. Had she left her computer on? The deposit out? She didn't think so. Closing was habit for her, and she did it the same way every night. Shelby opened the reception area door, but there was no light coming from the computer and no deposit bag on the table.

She must be going crazy. It was probably just the fear of not getting the money needed that had her freaking out. Opening the desk drawer, she placed her purse inside and then took off her coat. The chill set in immediately. She needed to get the heater turned on so the kids wouldn't freeze when they got here, and then maybe fix herself some hot tea.

The thermometer was located on the way to the kitchen, and she clicked it on and cranked the dial up a few notches for good measure. Then she turned on the kitchen light and grabbed the kettle from the stove. It still had a little water in it, but figuring she might need more, she took off the lid and placed it under the faucet. She turned the handle, but no water came out of the faucet. Shelby tapped on the handle. Was there a clog some-where? Had the landlord forgotten to pay the water bill?

No, she would have gotten a notice if that was the case, wouldn't she?

"Shelby? Are you here?" Tucker's voice carried through the quiet building.

"In the kitchen," she called back.

"Everything okay?" he asked as he stepped through the door frame.

"Not really. We don't seem to have water." She turned the faucet again to show him, and a frown creased his features.

"Do you know where the water shut off valve is?"

Shelby blinked at him. Water shut off valve? What was he talking about? She didn't have any water, so why would she need to shut it off. "I don't know. Why?"

"I think your pipes might be frozen, and if we don't get the water shut off before they start thawing, they could burst."

Shelby's eyes widened. Was this what her ominous feeling had been about? "That would be bad, right?"

"That would be very bad. Burst pipes usually cause flooding which could shut the center down for weeks."

"No! No, no, no." She shook her head as she began pacing the floor. "We can't shut down for weeks. If we shut down, we'll lose the last few clients we have, and then I'll have no way to pay the rent." She was babbling, but she couldn't stop it. This was her nightmare come true, and she'd thought they were finally going to be able to save the center.

"Shelby." Tucker grabbed her arms and stilled her pacing. "We can fix this, but I need to shut off the water. Is there a basement area?"

Basement? She tried to make her brain work; but not only was it still focused on the problem, it was also now reacting to Tucker's touch. Heat from his hands pulsated through her arms, and she felt mesmerized by his stare. "Basement?" This time she managed to say the word out loud. "Yes, I think there is."

"Okay, can you show me?"

Shelby nodded, blinked, and forced her mind to concentrate. "Yes, yes, of course." She led the way out of the kitchen and down the narrow hallway that led to the basement area.

"Wait here. I'll be right back."

As Tucker disappeared through the doorway, Shelby knotted her hands together and closed her eyes. She needed the peace that prayer brought.

Tucker made his way carefully down the narrow stairs. The last thing he needed was to fall and injure himself before the next game. He shivered as the air grew even colder and wondered if the basement was even insulated. No wonder the pipes had frozen.

His foot hit the floor and he glanced around the small room. Actually "room" might have been an overstatement. He could touch every wall from where he stood, but thankfully that made it easy to find the water valve. It creaked and groaned under his grip, but he managed to switch it off. Now, they just had to find a way to thaw the pipes without causing them to burst.

Not being a plumber, he didn't trust himself to know the best way to thaw them. Thankfully, he knew a plumber and one that owed him a favor. He made his way carefully back up the steps and found Shelby with her hands tightly clasped and her eyes closed. Her lips moved slightly as if praying.

He cleared his throat, not wanting to alarm her but wanting to let her know he was there. Her eyes snapped open.

"Did you find it?"

"I did, and I got it turned off. However, I'm no expert at this; and if we thaw them wrong, we could still cause them to burst. I recommend we call a plumber."

Her bottom lip folded under and sadness filled her eyes. Her hands twisted together, and her words tumbled out like an avalanche. "A plumber? But that will cost money. I don't have any money, and the landlord is on vacation until the end of the month. Plus, what if he can't come right away? We can't afford to close the center, but I can't have kids here if there's no water."

He crossed to her and placed his finger under her chin, lifting her eyes to his to get her attention. "Hey, I know a plumber who owes me a favor. Let me call him and see if he can come out. We'll figure out what to do from there."

She nodded, but his heart still went out to her. She looked so stressed, like anything else might send her screaming for the hills, and he wished he had a way to shoulder her worry. "I'll be right back, but trust me, it will be okay."

Tucker hoped he hadn't spoken too soon as he stepped away from her and dialed the number of his contact. It rang in his ear, and he clenched his jaw. "Come on, Teddy, pick up. I need you to pick up." He glanced back over his shoulder to make sure Shelby was still out of hearing range.

"Perfect Plumbing, this is Teddy. How can I help you?"

Tucker breathed a sigh of relief at the sound of Teddy's voice. "Hey, Teddy, it's Tucker Jackson. You remember that favor you owe me?" Tucker had run into Teddy at a fundraiser this past summer. The man had been desperate for tickets to the season opener for his son's birthday; and as Tucker had few friends at the time to invite, he had offered up his box seats in exchange for a favor in the future.

"Tucker Jackson. Of course, I remember. Bummer

about the loss the other night, but you guys will pull it out, right?"

"I sure hope." Tucker hated being reminded of the loss, but he knew Teddy meant nothing by it. It was something all fans said at some point as though they could commiserate with how hard the players trained only to still lose. "Anyway, I have a friend over at the community center. The snow froze their pipes, and we need to get them thawed so she can open today. You think you could squeeze in a little time to come check it out?"

"For you, man, I'll make some time. Let me get dressed and grab my tools. I'll be there in under an hour."

"Thanks, Teddy, you're a lifesaver." He punched the end call button and turned back to Shelby.

"Okay, he said he can be here in an hour."

"Thank you." She looked back toward the entrance. "Do you think we can still open? I don't want to turn people away, but I'd hate to let them in if we aren't going to have water."

"I'm sure he'll be able to get the water running again. What else do we need to do to prepare for the kids' arriving?"

Her brow furrowed as she thought. "Salt. We need to lay salt on the sidewalk."

"Okay, that's good. Do you have any here?"

"I think in the supply shed. Let me get the key and we can go check."

Tucker followed her back to the reception area and waited while she grabbed the key. He wondered when his view of her had shifted. When he'd first met her, he'd found her so stiff that he'd wondered if a rod had been jammed into her spine. She had looked as if she didn't know the meaning of the word relax much less how to do it; but over the last two days, he had seen her sense of humor and how much she cared for these kids. Now when he saw her, he didn't see stiff and unapproachable. Instead, he saw a strong woman who would do anything for those she cared about. And he found it attractive and appealing.

"Okay, got it," she said dangling the key in front of her face. "What?"

"Nothing." He couldn't tell her how he felt. Not yet anyway. He needed to know if she felt anything for him first, and he should probably wait until his time here was finished. It would be way too uncomfortable to continue working with her if he shared his feelings and she didn't reciprocate them, and he had to fulfill his hours. "Let's go."

Another car had pulled into the parking lot while they were inside, and disappointment flooded Tucker when he realized it was Kenzi. Shelby would probably send Kenzi with him to get the salt instead of going herself now.

"Hey, everything okay?" Kenzi asked as she stepped out of her car.

"The pipes are frozen so there's no water right now, but Tucker called a plumber to come check them out," Shelby returned. "We were just heading to the shed to see if there's any salt."

"I'll go with him to get the salt. You should stay out here and let parents know when they arrive," Kenzi said.

Tucker bit back his disappointment and shivered in his jacket. He'd rather go with Shelby, but right now, he just wished they could get moving. Already, the cold was seeping in through his jacket, and he needed to do something to warm up. He hoped Teddy arrived soon because he would have to leave for practice a little early with the icy roads, and he'd like to be here to discuss the price arrangement.

Shelby glanced at her watch and blew out a breath, sending a white vapor cloud into the air. "You're probably right, although I thought people would be arriving by now. I hope the snow isn't keeping them away." Shelby handed the key to Kenzi and then scanned the parking lot. "Can you see if there's a shovel as well? Maybe if we shovel it, they will come."

Tucker couldn't help the grin that sprang to his face at her allusion to the old Kevin Costner movie. There was that sense of humor again. Was that part of what was intriguing him now?

"Come on, Tucker. Let's see what we can find." Though she was not dressed for snow in her tight jeans and high heeled boots, Kenzi led the way confidently across the parking lot.

The supply shed appeared to be in decent shape on the outside, but Tucker wondered what they would find inside. He feared everything would be old and worn like it was in the center.

"Okay, let's see if there's salt and a shovel in here." Kenzi inserted the key into the lock on the door of the small shed and turned it. Tucker heard the distinctive click and then Kenzi was pulling the door open. The shed was packed from one end to the other and Tucker wondered how they found anything when they needed it.

"Ugh, he could at least keep it a little neater," Kenzi said as she scanned the contents. Her eyes flicked to the ceiling. "Great, no light either. Well, I guess just be super careful. Why don't you take that side, and I'll take this one?"

Without waiting for him to agree, she moved to the left and began scouring the shed. Tucker shook his head as he moved to the right. Visions of him tripping on something or stepping wrong and twisting his ankle flashed through his head. It would not do to get injured here.

"Here." He grabbed the handle of the sole shovel he saw leaning against the wall. It wasn't even a snow shovel which wasn't unusual as this area didn't receive snow that often, but it would make shoveling the snow a long and arduous process. "There's only one though unless you want to use a broom."

"I'm not sure a broom will do much good, but I found the salt. It's too heavy for me to lift, so if you can grab the salt, I'll take the shovel."

Tucker scanned the rest of the shed to see if there was anything else they could use, but while the shed was filled with all sorts of odds and ends, nothing looked as if it could move snow. He handed her the shovel, muscled the large bag of salt onto his shoulders, and followed her out of the shed.

9

The first car pulled in a few minutes later. With heavy shoulders, Shelby walked out to greet them.

"Is the center not open today?" the woman asked. Shelby recognized her as one of the more affluent moms who was now using the trampoline park down the street.

Shelby shook her head. "We will open, but unfortunately, our pipes froze. We're waiting on a plumber to thaw them. We have to wait until we have running water."

"So you don't even know if you'll open for sure?" Agitation filled the woman's voice as she glanced at her watch.

"I'm sorry. I know we'll open, but I don't have a specific time. I have no idea how long it takes to thaw pipes, but we can't have the kids have no access to water.

I'm sure you understand." Shelby tried to keep her tone even though frustration erupted in her at the woman's agitation. Here was a woman who barely used them anymore, yet she was angry that she couldn't drop her son off now when she was being inconvenienced by the snow.

The woman heaved an enormous sigh. "I do understand, and I guess I'll call later to see if you're able to open. Right now, I have to get to work as well." She turned to her son. "Guess it's grandma's for you today after all."

"Aw, Mom, Grandma's is so boring."

"Maybe it will only be for an hour or so. She can drop you back here if the place opens…"

Shelby didn't hear the rest of the conversation as the woman rolled up the window and drove away.

"It will be okay," Kenzi said, appearing behind her. She held a spade in her hand that didn't look as if it would do much good in the snow. "I'm sure the plumber is on his way, and Tucker has already started salting the sidewalk."

Shelby followed Kenzi's pointing hand to see Tucker shaking large salt pellets on the icy sidewalk as he stepped carefully toward the door. "Yeah, that's great, but will the plumber make it before other people show up and I have to tell them I have no idea when we'll open? What happens if they tell the other parents about the closure before we can get it fixed?" She turned as another car entered the parking lot and sighed. "Be right back."

"Hey, Shelby, is the center going to be open today?" This mom she recognized - Diana. Her ginger hair made it nearly impossible to not remember her, and Shelby had been surprised when she had pulled her sons. She'd thought they really enjoyed the center especially since both of them were planning to play basketball in high school.

"Morning, Diana." Shelby flashed her brightest smile, hoping it would ease any concerns Diana might have. "We do plan to open as soon as possible. Unfortunately, the snow froze our pipes, so we have no water right now. I've got a plumber on the way, and as soon as he thaws the pipes and we have water again, we'll open the center."

Diana's face tightened, and her smile wavered. Shelby knew that face. She'd seen it with every parent who had pulled their child. They'd flashed the patronizing, non-apologetic expression even as their words had tumbled out. "It's not you," they had said, but Shelby knew in a way it was. If she was more exciting, if she had more money, if she only had something to draw them in. . . And then a light went off in her head. She glanced back at Tucker who had evidently finished with the salt, taken the shovel from Kenzi, and now appeared to be attempting to move the snow with the less than ideal tool.

"I'm sorry, Shelby, I need to know they have a solid place to go this afternoon, and I won't have time to call and check."

Diana was a law clerk at the busiest law firm in the city, so not only was she probably late, but Shelby knew she would have a hard time getting away to bring the boys back. More than once, Shelby had been forced to call the backup number on the boys' sheet when she needed a quick response.

"Sure, I understand, but it would be a shame for the boys to miss the chance to hang out with Tucker Jackson." Shelby hoped she was hitting the nonchalant tone she was aiming for.

Diana's eyes lit up, and the corners of her mouth lifted again. "Tucker Jackson? From the Texas Tornadoes?" Her hand touched her throat as her eyes scoured the area for the star.

"Yep, he's come to help out at the center. Hoping to give back to the community and all. Have you seen the flyer about the clinic he's putting on tomorrow evening?" She bit her lip to keep from sharing any more excitement. She couldn't believe she had even said that much, especially since she had no idea for sure that the center would even be open tomorrow night. What if the pipes still burst before the plumber arrived?

The two blond boys in the back leaned forward, stretching against their seatbelts. "Mom, we have to come back and meet him. Please?"

Indecision crossed Diana's face, and she turned her slender wrist to check her watch. "Well, I guess I could stay for a little bit to see what the prognosis is. Work will probably make me stay late anyway."

"Yes." The exuberance in the boys' shout matched the feeling in Shelby's heart, and she forced herself not to join in with their cheer.

"Great, why don't you pull in over there." She pointed to the front row of spots that Tucker had somehow managed to clear out. "We should be able to get inside soon and then I can get you a flyer."

"They're staying?" Kenzi asked when Shelby returned to her friend's side.

"Yep." Shelby couldn't tame the smile that graced her lips. "I told them about our local football hero, and they decided to stay to see if the center will get to open. I guess they decided it might be worth the wait to spend the day with him."

10

Tucker glanced up as he felt eyes staring at him. Five cars were now parked in the lot waiting for the center to open. He hoped Teddy arrived soon because he would hate for Shelby to have to send the people away.

He tossed another trivial amount of snow to the side - he might as well have been using his hands at this rate - and then paused. Why did it feel as if the passengers in those cars were staring at him? Did they recognize him? He wasn't wearing any official team gear; and his coat, although fitted, was black and not flashy. Underneath, he wore jeans and a loose sweatshirt. Definitely not the attire that grabbed attention, and since he couldn't see inside the car windows, he had to assume they couldn't see his face well either. None of that abated the feeling though.

Relief flooded him when the plumbing truck pulled into the lot. Teddy. At last. Now, he could busy himself with helping the guy and escape the uneasy feeling. The truck pulled to a stop in front of him, the noise of the engine oddly loud in the otherwise quiet stillness. The engine idled for a moment as if the occupant did not want to step out of the warm embrace the heater offered, but then it too stilled and the silence returned.

The driver's door opened, and Teddy, wearing only a flannel shirt for warmth, stepped out of the cab. He was a large man, but Tucker found it hard to believe he wasn't freezing.

"Thanks for coming so quickly, Teddy," Tucker said, extending a hand.

"You're welcome though I have to tell you, I'm not usually up this early and certainly not when it's this cold outside."

"I hear you," Tucker said with a smile. "If you'll follow me inside, I'll show you the issue. I got the water shut off, but I have no idea how to thaw pipes."

"You shouldn't do it yourself anyway," Teddy said. "I've seen too many well-meaning homeowners flood their house trying to thaw pipes. Let me get my tools, and we'll see what we've got."

As Teddy returned to the truck, Tucker glanced at the parking lot again. There were now seven cars, and one was close enough that he could see the face of a child pressed against the glass. They were definitely here to see him. Well, he could tune them out. Just like during a game.

He'd always been able to do that - tune out the taunts along with the cheers. Probably because, after the first few times of looking, he'd realized his father wasn't in the stands - he was never in the stands - and he'd been the only one who mattered to Tucker. So, Tucker had just pretended the stands didn't exist. He'd pretended he was just playing with his friends in the park down the street like he had when he was eight and life was still easy. That had gotten him through high school and it would help him now.

"Okay, lead the way," Teddy said.

Tucker was only too happy to oblige. He turned his back on the peering eyes and led the way to the front door. "How is your son doing?" he asked as he pulled the front door open.

"He's good. Loved getting to watch the game from the luxury box. Thanks again for that."

"You're welcome. Listen, the director here is pretty strapped for money and the landlord is out of town at the moment. If I get you some tickets for next season's opener, do you think you could wait on payment?"

"I don't know, Tucker. It's Christmas and Jack wants some new Xbox game."

"I get that, but listen, I'm hosting a clinic here

tomorrow where I'll be teaching the kids some running plays and signing footballs and shirts. Everyone else is paying a hundred dollars to get in, but how about you bring Jack and consider your entrance fee your down payment? I promise you that the landlord is good for it, and you'll get the full amount when he gets back in town." He actually knew nothing about the landlord, but he trusted Shelby; and he couldn't see her working for someone underhanded.

"You'll sign whatever we want?" Teddy's eyes narrowed and he stroked his large chin thoughtfully.

"Whatever you want, Teddy."

"All right. You got yourself a deal, Jackson. You better work out your hand tonight though. I don't want it cramping in the middle of all that autographing."

Tucker smiled and clapped Teddy on the shoulder. "I'll do my best. Here's the door to the basement. It's pretty tight down there, but do you need some help?"

Teddy shook his head. "No way, man. I don't know what I'm going to find down there, and I am not going to be responsible for injuring Tucker Jackson during the play-offs. The mayor would probably yank my license. You know he's a fan."

Tucker nodded. The mayor attended nearly every game. "I do, but Teddy, I promise to be careful."

"No can do, Tucker. My license says all my guys have

to be bonded and insured. I doubt you are, but I promise I won't be long."

Tucker knew he wasn't going to win this argument. Teddy seemed like a good man, a rule follower, and Tucker wasn't going to push him to do something else. He would just have to return to shoveling and hope Teddy finished quickly.

Shelby turned at the tap on her shoulder.

"What did you tell these people, Shelby?" Tucker asked, motioning to all the cars. "I can feel them staring at me, and it's kind of creepy."

Shelby smiled. "Well, I mentioned to the first lady that you were going to be helping out this afternoon, and she decided to wait in hopes we open. I think she might be hoping to see you, and I'm fairly certain she called the other parents because it's been a steady stream since then."

"They're all waiting for me? Why?"

"I don't know. Maybe they're hoping to shake your hand or something, but this is great publicity for the event tomorrow. If we have this kind of turnout tomorrow, we should raise enough money for rent and the Christmas party, and I have no doubt these people will tell their friends."

Shelby smiled as she realized once again how in control God was. The snow had provided an excuse for Tucker to be seen outside. Not only that, but it had sent some of her previous families, who might not have known about the clinic, their way. But her smile faded as she remembered the pipes. If they weren't able to open tomorrow, all of this publicity would be for naught.

"Of course all of that hinges on if we can open. Did your friend say anything about the pipes?"

"Not yet, but he just started looking around down there. Give him a few minutes. He knows the situation and that you're in a time crunch."

Shelby nodded, but she couldn't keep the fear from constricting her voice. "Tucker, what am I going to do if he says we can't open? I don't have the money to keep this place open much longer."

Tucker placed a hand on her shoulder. "I don't think you'll have to worry about that. I know the center is old and in need of repair, but I have a feeling the rest of the pipes will be fine. Besides, the snow is letting up. Knowing Texas weather, the sun will be out in ten minutes and all of this will be melted by noon."

Shelby glanced at his hand on her shoulder. It was just a touch, a friendly touch, but her skin was on fire under his hand. She had felt the same heat earlier when he touched her face. Was she falling for him? She couldn't be. He was not her type, or more to the point, she was not his type; but the look he was giving her now and the one he had given her this morning? She didn't know what to make of them. But she couldn't think about that right now. She had a center to focus on, and she didn't need to be getting distracted by a romance. Unfortunately, that logic didn't slow her heart rate or even her breathing which suddenly felt restricted.

"Thanks, Tucker."

Her gaze met his, and the squeezing sensation on her lungs tightened. His eyes were so dark. So dark that she felt as if she were falling as she gazed into their depths. She couldn't remember the last time a man had affected her like this. Was he feeling something too?

"Okay, it looks like the rest of the pipes are okay." The plumber's voice interrupted the moment, and Tucker's hand dropped from her shoulder as he turned to face the man. Shelby blinked and tried not to focus on the cold spot that now pulsed where his hand had been.

"I've got a machine thawing what I can reach, and I've turned up the heat in the rest of the center to get the ones in the walls. I'd like to take a look around and see how we can insulate them better, so this doesn't happen again; but you can open. The water pressure will be a little low until all the ice melts, but you do have water."

"Thank you." Shelby checked her watch. It was nearly nine in the morning. She wasn't sure how the parents who had stayed had managed it, but she was certainly thankful.

After a final glance at Tucker, Shelby led the way back into the center. The heater was definitely working over time as she could feel the warmth caressing her before she made it to the reception area to remove her coat. She fired up the computer and grabbed the stack of flyers that sat neatly next to it.

Then she slid the window open that separated the reception area from the main gym and smiled at the line of people waiting to come in. "Okay, open for business." She handed a flyer to the first mother. "Will you be staying all day?"

"Definitely. Cooper is such a big fan." Evidently, his mother was too because the woman barely glanced at Shelby as she took the paper. Her eyes were locked on Tucker who was shaking hands with the children as they entered.

"Wonderful, well, that flyer has all the information about the clinic tomorrow night. Cooper could get some training and bring something to be autographed. It's one hundred dollars if you're not a monthly member, but you can save twenty-five if we get you signed up to use the center through January."

"Sure, that sounds great. Will Tucker be working here through that time?"

Shelby paused as she thought of how to answer. Tucker was required to spend twenty hours at the center, and he'd already fulfilled four of those hours. Even with only being able to get three or four hours a day, he'd be done with his obligation by the end of the week or early next week. That would take him through Christmas but definitely not through the entire month of January, and while she hoped he would decide to stay after that, they hadn't discussed it.

"I don't know, but I do know he'll be here through Christmas."

"Oh, okay, can I just pay for the rest of December then?"

Shelby's heart dropped but she forced her smile to remain pleasant. "Of course. I'll get that set up for you."

The next woman's response was nearly identical, as was the woman's after that. By the time, Shelby had handed out the flyers and registered the kids for afternoon care, she had ten more people who said they would continue through the end of the month, but no one who committed to staying longer. While she was grateful for the extra money, it begged the question of what she was going to do after Tucker was gone.

"Hey, I have to get to practice, but I'll see you at four."

She glanced up at Tucker who stood at the reception window. "Yes, of course, thanks for the help this morning."

"No problem." He flashed her a lopsided smile, tapped the counter, and then he was gone.

11

Tucker pulled into the parking lot of the stadium, glad to see it only half full. He wasn't late then; he'd been afraid he might be, having to drive slower than he normally would. Though the snow had stopped, the roads were still pretty slushy. Since Texas drivers rarely had to deal with snow, they were extra cautious, making the drive even slower than it had to be. A part of him wondered if they would even have practice today. Because it rarely rained and almost never snowed, the stadium only had a partial roof which meant the field might still be covered in snow. Even if it wasn't, it would probably be a soggy mess.

He grabbed his bag, locked his truck, and headed for the locker room; but as he reached the door, the unease pulled at his heart again. The guys had said nothing yesterday, but would they know today? Would Blaine tell them? A part of him didn't think so. After all, Blaine was the captain, and it was his job to make sure there was unity and harmony on the team. Spreading information, even if it was the truth, about a team member certainly wouldn't do that. But what if Blaine was tired of dealing with him? What if he saw this as a way to remove Tucker from the team? Sharing the information about his community service might create enough tension on the team to get him traded again.

Tucker took a deep breath and tried to clear his head. Blaine wasn't like that. He'd done nothing but be supportive to Tucker, so there was no reason to think he would change now. Besides, even if he did tell the other guys about the incident, Tucker would own up to it. He had been in the bar, and he could have refused to throw a punch. His actions were his alone, and he needed to stop passing the blame to others.

He opened the door, fully expecting the hum of conversation to hush as he entered, but it didn't. The men who were there gave him a head nod but no one shot him an accusatory gaze. He threaded his way to his locker and dropped his bag on the bench.

"How did it go at the center last night?" Blaine asked, coming up behind him.

Tucker sighed and glanced around the room. Blaine's voice was low, but he had been hoping to avoid discussing

the center. "It was fine. I aired up some balls and enter-
tained the kids for a while."

Blaine nodded. "Good. Glad to hear it. Just keep your
head down. No more fights, no more bars. Understand?"

Tucker had no desire to step in a bar again, but agitation stirred in his stomach at Blaine's words. He hated it
when Blaine acted like this. He hadn't had a father figure
in years, and he definitely didn't need Blaine trying to fill
the role. "Yeah, I got it, Blaine."

Blaine stared at him a moment longer before issuing a
curt nod. "Good. Suit up and be ready to go in ten. We've
got a long practice today, and only a few more days to get
prepared for the next game."

After donning his pads and practice jersey, Tucker
jogged out onto the field for practice. True to Texas form,
the snow had stopped; and the temperature had risen,
though it was still cold without his heavy jacket on. Most
of the snow had melted, leaving soggy ground beneath.
Whatever snow had remained on the field had been
cleared, but the moisture made the ground slick and
spongy beneath his feet just as he'd expected. A perfect
recipe for injury if he wasn't careful. He wished he'd left
the center sooner because his muscles were cold and tight
as well, but there was no additional time to warm up.

Rubbing his arms to get the blood circulating, Tucker
jogged over to the huddle where Blaine was giving the
directions for the day. "Okay, I want to run an 'up the

middle' and an 'off tackle.' The next team we're facing has the number one defense in the league, so our running game is going to be important. That being said, Jackson needs to remain healthy, so no tackles today. Touch only. Is that clear?"

The men nodded and Tucker took his place in the line. At the snap of the ball, he moved toward Blaine, took the ball, pocketed it in his arms, and ran up the middle of the line. He growled as his foot lost traction in the soft ground, and he stumbled before anyone had the chance to touch him.

"All right, let's try that again," Blaine hollered as Tucker stood up. Frustration raged through Tucker as he made his way back to the line of scrimmage. Mud coated the front of his pants and socks, and his shoes squished, making his feet even colder.

"You all right?" Blaine asked.

"Fine, let's just run it again." Tucker handed the ball to Blaine, wiped his hands on the cleanest part of his jersey, and took his place in the line once again.

"Hut," Blaine yelled, and Tucker took off once again. He tucked the ball and pushed through the middle line managing a measly five yards.

"Let's try an 'off tackle' this time," Blaine said as he held out a hand to help Tucker up.

Tucker nodded and took his place once again. This time when the ball snapped, he ran toward the right line after making sure the ball was secure in his arms. He broke through the line and was just about to kick his speed into gear when he felt a shove on his back. It wasn't that hard, really, but due to the slick grass, it sent him stumbling forward to the ground.

As if fuel had been poured on a flame, anger burned within him, and he jumped up to confront the guy who had pushed him. "What's your problem? Blaine said no tackles."

"I didn't tackle you. It was a touch, man, chill out."

"It was a shove, and you know it." Tucker pulled back his shoulders and moved until he was chest to chest with the other player.

"All right, enough," the coach said, jogging onto the field and interrupting the two men before it could escalate into a fight. "Tucker, take five. We'll run some passing plays while you cool off."

"I don't need to cool off. He needs to learn what a shove is."

"I said enough. Bench. Now."

Tucker narrowed his eyes at his teammate and then stalked off the field. As he sat on the bench watching the next few plays, he tried to slow his heart and calm his breathing. He'd been doing so well the last few days, so why did his temper have to flare up now? Even more importantly, what could he do to stop it?

"What's wrong?" Shelby asked as Tucker yanked open the front door. The scowl on his face reminded her of his first day, but she hadn't seen it since. He'd changed, at least when he was in the center.

"Tough practice," Tucker said, shaking his head. "What do you want me to do?"

"Come here and talk to me first. If you go out looking like that, you'll scare the kids away, and I'd like them to come back tomorrow." She was teasing, mostly, but she did worry about him being around the kids like this. They had enough worry on their plate without adding whatever was bothering him to it.

Tucker sighed but nodded, and a moment later, he had dropped his bag and plopped down in the chair across from her. "I'm sorry, Shelby. I probably should have told you this earlier, but I have this anger issue. It doesn't come up all the time, and I've been managing it with boxing classes; but after our last loss, I mouthed off to the quarterback. I don't even know why - it wasn't his fault, but sometimes I just can't seem to stop it. Today, it happened again. One of the guys pushed me a little too hard and sent me sprawling to the ground, and I almost lost it." He dropped his head into his hands. "I don't want to be so angry, but I have no idea how to stop it."

Shelby pursed her lips together and placed a hand on

his arm. She wondered if his anger issues had played a part in earning him community service. "Tucker, are you a believer?"

"You mean like a Christian?" he asked, raising his head.

"Yes, I mean like a Christian."

He shrugged and ran a hand across the back of his neck. "I don't know. I mean I guess I know there's a God, but I can't say I've been close with him. At least not since my mom died. We pretty much stopped going to church then."

His words hit Shelby like a brick, and she leaned back. No wonder he had anger issues. She'd seen it with other kids in the center who lost a parent or went through a messy divorce. Some retreated, some grew depressed, and some dealt with anger. She tried to think of the right words to say. "I'm sorry. I didn't know about your mom. How old were you?"

His hand moved from his neck to his chin. "Twelve. Much younger than any boy should be. Plus, my dad withdrew into his work after that, and I pretty much had to raise myself and my sister."

Shelby blinked back the tears stinging her eyes. "Tucker, it's no wonder you're angry then. That is more than any child should have to deal with, but you don't have to deal with it alone. I know it's not the same because you can't see Him or touch Him, but God is your Father too, and He loves you. More importantly though, He can help you tame your anger and find forgiveness."

Tucker's hand stilled and his eyes locked on hers. "Do you really believe that? You really think He can take away my anger?"

She touched his arm again. "I know he can. I've seen him do it. My mom was just like that when I was growing up. She would get angry over every little thing. So angry that I used to hide under my desk when she would scream and yell. It was the only place that felt safe. And then one day, she just stopped. She stopped being mad all the time, and she turned into this amazing woman. I didn't ask her about it for a long time because I was afraid I might remind her and she would start yelling again; but one day, I got up the courage. She told me that God took her anger away. That she prayed for peace, and He gave it to her. Now, I know your situation might be a little different, but if God can do that for my mother, then I know He can do it for you as well."

Tucker held her gaze a moment longer and then nodded. "I believe you, but I'm not sure I know what to do."

"I could pray for you," she said softly. "If you want."

He took a deep breath, and Shelby forced herself to remain quiet while he thought. Then his hand covered hers, and the corners of his lips turned up. "I'd like that."

Warmth flooded Shelby as she closed her eyes. She

hadn't been sure he would be open to it, but she was delighted that he was. "Lord, I want to thank You for being a good Father to us. I know it isn't always easy for us to put our trust in things we cannot see, but I know that You can deliver peace. My friend Tucker needs that peace. Please take away his anger and help him find forgiveness. Also, help him to see You. Amen."

Shelby opened her eyes, unsure of what she would see, but Tucker's face appeared softer, less rigid. "Thanks, Shelby. I am sure that I still have a lot to learn, but I do feel better. Now, what can I do to help tonight?"

"Well, I think Kenzi and Jennifer, our high school volunteer, could use some help with the kids. What do you say we go find them?"

"Sounds good."

"Ah, there's the star of the day," Kenzi's voice carried across the gym as Shelby and Tucker approached. "Who wants Tucker to play hide-and-seek with us?"

The kids cheered and the sound warmed Shelby's heart. She sneaked a glance at Tucker and saw that he was smiling as well. He probably didn't even know it, but being around these kids was helping him too. Changing him.

"I haven't played hide-and-seek for years," Tucker said, rubbing his hands together. "I bet I can find some good spots though. You coming, Shelby?"

Shelby shook her head. "You go ahead. At least one of us needs to stay out here and be the adult. Just in case."

"Suit yourself," Tucker called as he headed toward Kenzi and the kids.

For a moment, Shelby envied Kenzi. How was she able to be so carefree and not seem to care about responsibility? It had been this way as long as Shelby could remember. She'd been the focused one in high school, worrying about grades and studying every night. Kenzi had been the one attending parties and cramming the night before tests. In college, Shelby had only joined the studious sororities while Kenzi had joined the ones who partied. Kenzi represented the side that Shelby would never be, and she supposed that was why they worked. They were like yin and yang, like peanut butter and jelly, complete opposites who complemented each other and together made a force to be reckoned with.

Still, that didn't mean Shelby didn't want to have fun now and then. She wished she could let loose and play with the kids too like she used to, but if she didn't stay in control, if she didn't keep a tight eye on the center, she knew it would go up in flames. And that was something she couldn't let happen. It was too important to the kids, especially the kids like herself who hadn't been born into affluent households and couldn't afford the latest gadgets and gimmicks.

With a sigh, Shelby returned to the reception area and pulled out the list of businesses she had canvassed earlier this afternoon. Thankfully, Jennifer had been truly under the weather yesterday, and feeling better, she had come in this morning shortly after Tucker left. That allowed Shelby to leave the center for a few hours to pass out flyers and beg for donations. Unfortunately, she hadn't been able to secure any, but the interest for the clinic had been high.

She had saved the center for the day, maybe even through January if everyone showed up tomorrow night, but they still had a long way to go. Plus, there was the Christmas party; she still needed to find a donor to help out with that. Their regular guy had been strangely silent so far this year. Perhaps a reminder call would help.

She had just picked up the phone when the front door opened. Sylvie Sanders from the channel five news floated in looking just as perfect as she did on television. Her blonde hair flowed like golden silk around her shoulders as if some invisible wind kept it aloft, and her figure was the perfect hourglass in her smart, tailored suit. A man holding a large camera entered behind her.

"Can I help you?" Shelby had no idea why Sylvie and her cameraman might be at her center. Had they heard about the clinic? Or about Tucker? It was possible but highly unlikely. It made more sense that they were lost though how people got lost today with maps on their phones was beyond her.

"Yes, we heard that Tucker Jackson was working here and was holding a clinic tomorrow night, is that correct?"

So, they were here for Tucker. Had the newspaper

called them? Or maybe Tucker's PR guy had - she had forgotten to even ask him about that today. Either way, she supposed she shouldn't look a gift horse in the mouth - the center could definitely use the publicity - but it would be nice to have somebody do a story on the center just because it helped out the local kids and not because a pro athlete was around for the week. "He's volunteering here, yes." Shelby hoped the smile on her face didn't look as fake as it felt.

"Wonderful. Could we talk with him? This has feel-good story written all over it." Sylvie's words were as smooth and polished as her appearance, but they were hollow and empty. Shelby wondered if the woman even knew what a feel-good story was.

"Sure. Let me see if I can find him. They're playing hide-and-seek, so it may take me a moment." Why was she trying to discourage this? This was just the kind of publicity the event needed. But she knew why. It was because Sylvie was the epitome of perfection. She was blonde, beautiful, and the type of trophy woman that a professional athlete would want to show off on his arm. She even made Kenzi seem average which made Shelby feel even more invisible. So, while she appreciated the news running the story, she just wished someone other than Sylvie Sanders was covering it.

Sylvie's perfect eyebrows arched on her wrinkle-free forehead, and her lips twisted into a condescending smile.

"Hide-and-seek? In this place?" Her nose turned up at the last two words as if she couldn't believe she had to stand in this building. "Why don't you just call him on his cell? Surely that would be faster."

It would be faster, and Shelby had his number; but there was a part of her that wanted to make Sylvie wait. The woman looked as if she never had to wait, as if everything she wanted in life was delivered to her on a silver platter at the snap of her finger. No, not a silver platter, she probably had a golden one. The perfect fourteen carat gold to match the tiny hoops in her ears and the delicate bracelet on her slender wrist. So, yeah, she could wait.

"It might be faster, but we discourage cell phone use at the center. We want the adults to be engaged with the children, and we've found that devices are distracting, so we don't allow cell phones except for emergencies." It wasn't exactly the truth, but it wasn't a flat out lie either. It was the policy Shelby herself followed, and she had asked Kenzi and Tucker not to have their phones out when the kids were around; but there was no strict policy. She felt a little guilty fibbing to Sylvie, but she pushed it aside.

"I'm sure it won't take me very long to find him." Shelby mirrored Sylvie's condescending smile before exiting the room to begin her search. As she crossed the big gym, she felt very conspicuous in her bargain store pants and blouse. She normally considered herself a smart dresser; she always looked professional even if her clothes were purchased second hand, but next to Sylvie, she could have been the poster child for dowdy.

Tucker wasn't in the kitchen or in the hallway. Where could he be hiding? She felt like time was speeding by and dragging at the same time. If it took too long, would Sylvie leave? Would she do a story about how terrible the manager was? Shelby quickened her pace, determined not to find out.

She pulled open the door to the supply closet and sighed in relief when she saw Tucker inside.

"Shut the door," he said. "You're going to give me away."

"Sylvie Sanders from channel five is here. She wants to interview you."

His eyes lit up. "Sylvie Sanders? The blonde?"

Shelby shrugged. Was his excitement over the interview or the woman conducting it? She shouldn't care; he hadn't expressed an interest in her. At least not in words. But there'd been moments. Moments where she thought he felt something for her, and imagining him with Sylvie felt wrong. Yes, on the surface, they worked with their good looks and perfect jobs; but there was more to Tucker than the stereotypical athlete who always dated the modelesque women. At least, she had thought there was, but maybe she'd been wrong. "That's the one."

"Lead the way then."

Shelby led him back to Sylvie and tried not to grimace when Sylvie batted her eyes at Tucker.

"Tucker Jackson. A little birdie told us you were working here. Do you mind telling us what you're doing in a place like this?"

Shelby bristled at Sylvie's insinuation. Yes, the place needed sprucing up, but it wasn't like it was a landfill or a deathtrap the way Sylvie was making it sound.

Tucker glanced at Shelby before pasting a smile on his face and turning his charm on. "I wanted to give back to the community."

Oh, brother. Shelby rolled her eyes as she made her way back to the reception area. It wasn't like she expected him to admit he was only here to serve community service hours, but she hadn't thought he would lay it on so thick. Shelby hoped this interview brought some good publicity to the center and didn't backfire on her. The last thing she needed was anything else to go wrong.

12

"So, how did we do?" Kenzi asked as Shelby closed out the register.

"Not bad. Thankfully, the landlord will cover the pipes when he returns, and I think we made enough today to pay January's rent. At least we will if the clinic is a success tomorrow night as well."

"Well, that's good. Thank goodness Tucker Jackson came along when he did, right?" Kenzi had that annoying lilt in her voice - the one she used when she was trying to persuade someone to do what she wanted - but Shelby was immune. She'd become Kenzi's friend because she enjoyed hanging out with her not because she'd been sucked in by the charms that seemed to make anyone else fall under her spell.

Shelby shrugged. "I guess. I mean he's certainly been

helpful, but we'll have to see how tomorrow goes." She placed the money in the pouch and zipped it closed.

Kenzi rolled her eyes. "He's been amazing and you know it. This is about that reporter, isn't it?"

Heat flamed across Shelby's cheeks, and she turned away as if looking for something. She hated that Kenzi knew her so well, hated that she was envious of the reporter. Or maybe not the reporter per se, but the way Tucker had interacted with her. He'd been charming and smiley, almost flirtatious. Maybe it had just been to get a good interview, but she was no longer sure. She'd thought Tucker had connected with her, opening up about his anger and letting her pray for him; but apparently, she'd been wrong. "It's not about the reporter though did you see the way he acted? Those two deserve each other. Probably both hung up on their money and good looks."

"Oh. My. Gosh. You like him."

"What?" Shelby turned back to Kenzi to see her wide eyes sparkling.

"You like him. Tucker Jackson. You think he's cute."

"I don't... He's not..." Shelby blew out a frustrated breath. "Okay, fine, I think he's cute, who wouldn't? But it's not like it matters. I am not the type of girl that a guy like Tucker notices. He notices girls like you and Slyvie Sanders."

"I think you're being entirely too hard on yourself. You have a lot to offer a man like Tucker."

Shelby cocked her head at her friend. "Wait, I thought you liked Tucker. Why does it sound like you are trying to convince me to give him a shot?"

Kenzi shrugged. "I like the idea of Tucker, and yes, he is easy on the eyes, but I think he's looking for something more than I can offer him. I was telling him last night that I didn't know what I wanted to do for a job, and he got this funny expression on his face. And then he looked toward the office. Where you were."

A weird feeling that straddled the fence somewhere between embarrassment and denial erupted in Shelby. "I doubt he was looking at me." Except they'd had that moment yesterday. That moment where he'd lifted her chin, and she thought some spark passed between them. And then more moments earlier today. But then there was Sylvie and the way he acted with her. Shelby didn't didn't know what to think.

Kenzi's lips twisted into a teasing smile. "I'll take that bet. I think you're wrong about him, and if you'd let me do a little makeover on you, I could get him to notice you the same way he did Sylvie. You're beautiful, Shelby. You just hide it."

Shelby lifted her chin and clenched the money bag tighter. "I don't need a makeover. If a man doesn't like me for who I am, then he isn't the man for me."

"Famous last words of the spinster," Kenzi said with a smile.

Shelby marched over to the door and flicked off the lights. "I will not be a spinster."

"Who's a spinster?"

Shelby jumped at the sound of Tucker's voice behind her and nearly dropped her keys. She hadn't known he was still in the center. "No one. What are you still doing here? I thought you left."

"I needed to see you first. Do you think I could skip coming in the morning tomorrow? They moved practice up, and I'd like to spend the few hours before it hammering out what I want to show the kids. I can make up the missed time next week."

"Sure, that would be fine. How did the interview go?" Shelby wasn't sure she wanted to hear his answer, but the question came out anyway.

He cocked his head at her and smiled. "It was fine. Sylvie seems very nice. A little high maintenance but nice. Anyway, I'll see you tomorrow." He grabbed her hand and squeezed it. "Thank you for earlier. I'm going to take your advice."

Shelby watched him walk out of the center and then turned when she heard Kenzi cough behind her.

"See? I told you he likes you."

"No," Shelby shook her head, "that was nothing. He was just thanking me."

Kenzi's brow lifted. She was not convinced. "Uh huh, well he held your hand while he thanked you which wasn't necessary. I would say there's something there. If he asks, would you date him?"

"I - I don't know. I mean we're so different. What if it doesn't work out?"

"What if it does?"

Shelby had no answer to that. She'd only had a few steady boyfriends, and they had all seemed to become bored with her long before they even thought of proposing to her. Could Tucker be different? Was there something to the old saying that opposites attract?

Tucker woke with a start to the light coming in his window. What time was it? He opened his eyes and groaned. Eleven? Shelby had allowed him to take the morning off to prepare for the clinic tonight, but he had planned to work on the plays he wanted to show the kids. However, somehow he had slept through his alarm. He was supposed to be suiting up for practice right now. Why hadn't anyone on the team called him? Frustrated, he punched the home button to wake his phone only to see Blaine had called him. Twice. He must have been so exhausted from yesterday that he slept through the alarm and through the calls.

He punched the number to return the call as he jumped out of bed and began grabbing clothes for a shower. "Blaine? It's Tucker," he said when the quarter-back answered.

"Tucker, how nice of you to return my call. You do realize you are supposed to be here getting ready for practice, right?" The tone in his voice rubbed at Tucker's irritation, but he forced himself to remain calm.

"I do. I'm sorry man, but I am on my way. Just give me half an hour to take a shower and grab some food, and I'll be there."

"I know this center work is throwing off your hours, but missing practice could get you benched for the next game."

Tucker pinched his lips together as the frustration bubbled within him. Blaine was infuriating. Yes, it was his fault for being late, but if Blaine only knew how hard he worked last night. He'd had no idea playing with kids would require so much energy, so much mental effort. Blaine probably didn't either. The man most likely didn't even have family; he was probably some amazing AI unit as perfect as he was. Tucker was about to issue a snide retort when Shelby's words from yesterday flashed in his mind. Though he wasn't sure he was ready to come back to God fully, he was prepared to try. He issued a silent prayer, hoping that God would understand his hesitation, and then took a deep breath. "I understand Blaine. I'll be right there."

He jumped into the shower, wishing he had more time

to enjoy the warm pelts of water. For as long as he could remember, he'd enjoyed showers. The heat, the steam, the feel of the water washing away the old. His favorite part was watching the cloud of steam roll out and fog the mirrors when he was done. It made him feel a little like a rockstar. His mother had often teased him that he would be the death of her with his hot water bill.

His mother. Was Shelby right? Was his mother's death still affecting him a decade later? Would he ever stop feeling sadness and anger over her unjust and untimely death? He washed the last of the soap out of his hair and turned off the water. The hot water hadn't even been on long enough to create steam.

He regarded his reflection in the mirror and wondered how different he might be if his mother hadn't died, if his father hadn't thrown himself into his work, if Tucker hadn't had to become the parent for both him and his sister. Would he even be in this situation? Somehow he doubted it. He doubted he would have been as angry, and, therefore, he probably wouldn't have been in the bar. Maybe he wouldn't have even been traded.

But, it was no use living in the past. His mother was gone and life was what it was. What he needed to do now was to focus on the present. Get to practice. Finish his sentence at the center. Win the championship. Give his anger to God?

Shelby's words from yesterday floated through his

mind again. Could God really take his anger away? It had seemed to lessen after he prayed, so could there be something to it? Could He help Tucker forgive his father? He supposed it was possible, but he didn't have the time to think more about it right now. Right now, he had to focus on getting to practice before he got benched for the rest of the season.

13

"Excuse me, but when is this going to start?" A woman bouncing a baby in her arms asked from the front row. The scowl on her face matched several others throughout the crowd.

Shelby stared out at the sea of faces filling the gym. She should be happy to see this many people here. And she was. Except there was one face missing. The face that really needed to be here. Tucker's. Where was he?

She'd called him half an hour ago when he missed the set up time and then again ten minutes ago when the families began arriving, but she'd gotten his voicemail both times. She'd let him have the morning off to prepare, but surely he hadn't forgotten or flaked on her. She'd been under the impression he was at least a man of his word.

"Sorry I'm late." His loud voice quieted the din

momentarily, and then the kids went crazy when they realized who it was. He crossed the room to Shelby's side and whispered the apology again in her ear. "I'm so sorry."

A tingle shot down her spine as his breath tickled her ear. "You know, even volunteers are supposed to show up on time." Shelby kept her voice low, but she arched her left eyebrow as she waited for whatever lame excuse he was going to throw at her.

His mouth pinched into a tight line. "Yeah, I know, practice ran long even though it was supposed to end early."

"I get that, Tucker, but these kids depend on us. When we say we are going to do something, we have to follow through."

"I know," he said. "I do, and I brought some new balls to make up for it." He held up a bag. "Now, how do you want me to get this started today?"

She wasn't really done reading him the riot act, but she supposed she should show a little grace since he had brought balls and a ton of new kids into the center. "I'll introduce you, and you can take it from there. Sound good?"

He nodded, and Shelby held out her hand to quiet the room again. "Are you guys excited?" she asked.

"Yes!" The yells of the room nearly pushed her back. They were definitely excited.

"Did you bring something for Tucker to sign? If you did, hold it up."

Around the open area, arms popped up with footballs, t-shirts, and other items clutched in their hands.

"All right, you guys look ready, so I'm going to hand the floor over to Tucker Jackson of the Texas Tornadoes."

More yelling and clapping raised the decibels another level, and Shelby felt like she was back at the one rock concert she had attended in college. It had been Kenzi's idea. Concerts weren't really Shelby's thing; and after nearly losing her hearing for a day following the noise fest, she had never attended another one.

She watched for a moment as Tucker introduced himself, hoping he was a decent speaker. Her fears proved unfounded though as he held the room's attention even as he began explaining how the clinic would go. Inch by inch, Shelby backed up until she felt she was far enough back not to be a distraction, and then she turned and walked back to the office.

With a sigh, she sat down at the small desk and pulled out the few cards they had on donors. She didn't like using Tucker's name, but maybe if she mentioned he was here for the rest of the month, they might be more willing to donate.

The first name on the list was Lydia Benson. Lydia had been a local designer before her business took off and she moved to New York. She would probably be too busy

- that's the excuse she had used last year and the year before - but Shelby had to try. Maybe reminding the woman of her roots and reminding her of the tax break might help.

"Lydia's Designs, how can I help you?"

Shelby didn't recognize the nasally, professional voice on the other end of the phone, but she knew it wasn't Lydia herself. The woman had always had a lilt to her voice that oozed high society even before she joined their ranks. "Yes, is Lydia available? This is Shelby Doll."

"Shelby Doll?" The voice paused as if searching her memory or a computer. "Are you a designer?"

"Uh, no. I run the community center in Southlake, Texas, her hometown."

"Oh." Immediately, the tone of the voice on the other end shifted. The polite professionalism was replaced with bored impatience. "I'm sorry. She's very busy right now with her new line. You can give me your number, and I'll make sure she gets the message."

"Yeah. Sure." Shelby doubted her number would ever cross Lydia's desk. One down and only three to go. What would she do if she received the same response from the rest of them? She closed her eyes and issued a prayer.

The next name was Dr. Bill Gaines. He probably wouldn't be able to come to the phone either. As the prominent surgeon in Southlake, he was usually either in surgery or golfing, but he'd grown up in the center, so she knew he had a soft spot for it. She dialed the number on the card and held her breath.

"Surgical Institute of Southlake, how may I direct your call?"

"Hi, this is Shelby Doll with the community center. I was hoping I might speak with Dr. Gaines."

"I'm sorry Dr. Gaines is in surgery. Would you like to leave a message?"

She didn't want to leave a message. Messages could be ignored, avoided, forgotten. She wanted to speak to a live body, to work her persuasive magic, but she was striking out today. "Yes, thank you. I'll leave a message." Perhaps, she could be charming enough on his machine that he would return her call or at least be open to speaking to her when she called again.

Shelby twirled the blonde strand of hair that always escaped her updo as she listened to his voicemail. When she heard the beep, she sat straighter in her chair and smiled brightly. She'd felt silly in college when they'd had to practice smiling on phone calls. No one could even see her, but after listening back to the calls, she'd had to agree that a smile came through the phone in the brightness of the tone. And every salesperson knew that a friendly tone was half the battle of getting a sale. Or in her case, a donation.

"Hello, Dr. Gaines, this is Shelby Doll from the South-lake Community Center. I know you are very busy, but I also know this center was a large part of your life growing up. We are looking for donations for our annual Christmas party, and I know the kids would love to see your name on the sign. You are such an inspiration to them, and remember that every dollar donated is tax deductible. Please give me a call at 555-7663 so we can deliver some cheer to the youth of Southlake."

She let her smile fade as she hung up the phone. Just two names left. Could she manage to get one of them on the line, or was she going to have to go door knocking again tomorrow to find new donors?

"Lord, please," she prayed softly as she picked up the next card. "We need a miracle."

Tucker stared at his reflection in the cloudy mirror and sighed. He looked exhausted and he'd only been here a few hours. He was enjoying teaching the kids, and he still had the signing to do; but he'd needed a break from the noise for a minute. He understood now why people worked with kids. There was something rewarding in their smiles, their energy; but he did not understand how people dealt with the noise. The kids seemed to have never heard of volume control, and they would ask questions on top of each other. Did they really think he couldn't hear them when he was five feet away? And why didn't their parents intercede? Most of them were in the room, congregating against the wall and on their phones, but in the room.

Perhaps the phones were the problem. He knew some of them were recording their child participating in the clinic, but the others? Some of them never even looked up as their kid caught the ball and ran the routes he had taught them. It made him wonder if the kids were just as invisible at home, and the thought tugged on his heart. That he could definitely relate to.

He splashed cold water on his face and made a mental note to bring Tylenol if they ever did this type of event again. The pounding in his head didn't appear to be subsiding any time soon. He grabbed a paper towel from the dispenser and sighed when he realized it was the last one. He'd have to ask Shelby to replace it. Or maybe Kenzi. She'd been helping him out with wrangling the kids.

He tossed the paper towel in the trash and exited the bathroom, but before he reached the gym, the sound of muffled voices reached his ears. He turned the corner to see a beefy, muscular kid poking a boy in a wheelchair. The boy in the wheelchair was a regular, Benji, but the other boy he didn't recognize. He strained to hear the conversation, but the words were too soft to hear. However, the body language was easy to read.

"Hey, what are you two doing out here? You're supposed to be in the main gym."

The beefy kid turned to face him. An insincere expression of apology masked his face, and Tucker knew he was about to get fed a story. "Sorry, we got lost looking for his book, right man?" He looked back at Benji as if daring him to contradict the story.

Benji's eyes dropped to his lap, and his shoulders stooped as if weighed down with defeat. He was probably used to getting bullied. "Yeah, I think I dropped it somewhere and Colson here was helping me look for it."

Tucker had no doubt that was the furthest thing from the truth, but it was clear from Benji's reaction that he didn't want to disobey Colson. Tucker had seen enough bullies in action to know that's what was going on here, and he was not going to let it continue. Benji was a great kid, one of his favorites, but he needed to know the details before he took any further action.

"Okay, well I'll help Benji find his book. You go on and head back to the gym, Colson. You can tell them I'll be right there."

Colson opened his mouth as if to object. His eyes shifted from Tucker to Benji, clearly trying to decide if Benji would rat him out once he was gone.

"Don't worry, I'll be sure to tell everyone how helpful you were," Tucker said.

Colson closed his mouth, and after another long stare at Benji, he headed back toward the gym.

Tucker waited until he was sure Colson was out of

earshot before approaching Benji. "You want to tell me what that was about?"

Benji rubbed his hand across his neck before folding it in his lap again. "Just what we said. I lost my book. Colson was helping me look for it."

Tucker knelt down in front of the boy. "Benji, I know that isn't the truth. I couldn't hear what was said, but I could tell from his posture and your reaction that he was being aggressive. Now, I want to help you, but I can't do that unless I know why."

Benji's bottom lip folded under, and unshed tears glistened in his eyes. "He told me that my father left because I was a cripple, that no father wants half a son."

Tucker clenched his jaw to keep the anger boiling within him from spilling over. He would save it for Colson and chew the kid's ear off, but this boy needed compassion. After taking a deep breath to calm his words, Tucker touched Benji's arm. "First of all, Colson was wrong. I don't know why your father left, but I'm sure it had nothing to do with you."

Benji shrugged and sniffed back the tears Tucker was sure were pressing against his eyes.

"Look, do you think I'm the type of son a father would want, at least according to Colson?"

"Of course." Benji's lips split into a wide smile. "You're a pro-football player, and I'll never be that. What kind of dad wouldn't want a pro player as a son?"

"Mine." As soon as Tucker uttered the word, he realized how profoundly his father's lack of engagement had affected him. "See, my mom died when I was about your age, and my dad disconnected. Threw himself into work. Do you know he's never even seen one of my games in person? I don't even know if he watches them on TV."

Benji's mouth fell open. "Seriously? But...but you're Tucker Jackson."

Tucker chuckled. "Yeah, but that doesn't matter to my dad. Sometimes dads just mess up. They aren't perfect either." He paused as he realized how true that was and how misplaced his anger at his father had been. Shelby was right. "I think I thought my father's avoidance was because he no longer loved me, but talking with you, I realize that he is just human. He's dealing with his own pain, and my pain was just an unfortunate consequence of that."

"So, my dad might have left even if I wasn't different?"

The raw hope in Benji's voice tugged at Tucker's heart, and he nodded. "I'm certain that your father left because of his own issues and not because of you." Tucker felt that was the truth. Even if Benji's father had left because of his handicap, that action showed that he had some deeper issue he was dealing with or perhaps unable to deal with.

"Thank you, Mr. Jackson. I think I can go back now."

"You're welcome, and you can call me Tucker, Benji. All my friends do."

Benji smiled so brightly that even the corners of the room appeared to light up, and warmth flooded Tucker's heart. This was almost better than winning football games and hearing the crowd going wild. Maybe he could see why Shelby worked a job like this, even with the noise. Shelby. He would need to tell her she was right and talk to her about how to handle Colson, but he had to finish this clinic first.

"Okay, guys," he said, stepping back into the crowd. "Did you guys all have fun?" The answer was a resounding roar of voices and clapping of hands. "Great, I'm so glad. I have some time to sign autographs before we wrap up for the night, so if you could form a single line, I'll sign whatever you brought."

He wasn't sure the kids would be able to handle the directions, but thankfully Kenzi helped herd them into something resembling a line while he took his place at the table. One at a time, he signed footballs, shirts, books, stickers - whatever was passed across the table to him - until all the kids were taken care of. With the last item signed and the kids packing up and leaving, he shook out his cramping hand and looked around for Shelby.

There was still no sign of Shelby, but he saw Kenzi speaking to a woman at the front door. Perhaps this would be a good time to find Shelby and tell her about the

Colson incident. He saw neither boy in the few who remained.

Tucker wandered over to the reception area and was about to rap lightly on the doorframe when he heard Shelby's voice from inside.

"Please, Mr. Renfrow, if you could just tell me why. Maybe it's something we can remedy."

Renfrow? Why did that name sound familiar?

He waited a moment longer for her to finish the call. It felt like eavesdropping though that wasn't his intent. When he heard Shelby sigh, he figured she had hung up with whomever had been on the other end, and he poked his head in the doorway. "Hey, you got a minute?"

"What is it?" There was a note of defeat in her voice that he hadn't heard before, and he wondered if it was due to the phone call.

He leaned against the doorframe, keeping a professional distance between them even though he wanted to touch her. "I just wanted to tell you the boy's bathroom is out of paper towels and get some feedback on how to deal with a bullying situation, but if you're busy, we can discuss it tomorrow."

She let out another sigh which sounded as if it carried the weight of the world on its shoulders. "No, it's fine. I need a break from calling donors anyway."

"Sorry, I didn't mean to overhear, but was that a donor on the phone just now?"

"Yeah. Jude Renfrow. He's a local investor. Donated for the Christmas party last year, and I thought he was on board this year, but now he says some recent event has changed his mind."

Jude Renfrow. Suddenly, Tucker knew why that name sounded familiar, but he forced his face to remain impassive. The last thing he needed was Shelby knowing that Jude's sudden change of heart was his fault.

"Anyway, that's not your burden," Shelby said with a wave of her hand. "Tell me about this bullying incident."

Tucker relayed the incident to her and watched as her face shifted from concern to anger and then back to its professional demeanor. He could tell that she tried not to dislike any of the kids in the center, but she definitely did not like bullying behavior.

"I think I made Benji feel better," Tucker continued, "but I'm not sure what to do next."

Shelby crossed the file cabinet and pulled out Colson's file. She flipped it open. "There isn't much on him; he's never been a regular, just dropped in once in a while. To be honest, he's probably only here now because of you, but we need to document it. If it continues," she opened a different drawer and pulled out a documentation form, "I'll have to reach out to his parents. If he shows up tomorrow, let's try to keep them separated and definitely make sure Benji is never alone with him. I'll tell Kenzi to keep an eye out too." She handed him the form.

He took it and began filling out the report. "The event went well. Do you think you earned enough money?"

"I don't know. I hope so, but I'm afraid we still won't have enough for the party. I hate not being able to give that to the kids."

"How about you let me take care of that?" Tucker asked as he finished filling out the form and passed it back to her. "I'll come in early tomorrow and we can discuss what you need, and I'll take care of the funding."

Shelby's brow furrowed with questions. "Why would you do that? I thought this was just community service for you."

"It was. When I started, but these kids have grown on me." He grabbed her hand and pulled her close to him. "You have grown on me."

Her eyes widened as she gazed up at him.

"You were right, Shelby. I was angry because of my mother's death, and I was angry that I thought my father didn't love me either, but Benji helped me see that's not the case. I've been praying when I feel the anger rise, and God's been helping me. You've helped me. I didn't want to say anything while I was still serving hours in case you didn't feel the same, but I'd really like to take you out. Maybe tomorrow night after we close?"

He could almost feel the pounding of her heart in the air, and a soft electric buzz seemed to surround them. "I'd like that," she finally whispered.

"Good." His eyes traced the soft curve of her lips, and his breath caught. Every ounce of his body wanted to kiss her, but it didn't seem to be the right time or place. Besides, Kenzi or a parent could walk in on them at any moment. "Now, should I replace those paper towels before I leave?"

She blinked at him, clearly startled by the change in subject. "Of course," She grabbed a key off the rack on the wall and handed it to him. "Here's the key to the supply closet. You should find some there and you can replace them."

"Thanks, I'll take care of this."

Shelby stared at the doorway long after Tucker had gone. What had happened there? He'd asked her out on a date, she'd thought he was going to kiss her, and then he'd veered back to the paper towels. Perhaps, he just wanted to remain professional at work? She could understand and respect that. At least logically. It was a lot harder to tell her heart that.

"You all right?" Kenzi asked from the doorway.

"Yeah, just thinking." Should she tell Kenzi about the date? She knew her friend would be happy, but there was still a part of Shelby that didn't believe it was real. Maybe she could wait until tomorrow night to tell her, just to be sure.

"How'd we do?" Kenzi asked.

"Good. Enough to pay for January's rent and a little extra. I couldn't get any of the donors, but Tucker said he'd fund the party."

"He did, huh?" Kenzi's voice held that teasing lilt again. She fell into step as Shelby walked to the front door. "You know, he's pretty good with the kids too."

"Yeah, he seems to be. It's too bad he's only here for another week though because we are still behind on money."

Kenzi offered a crooked smile as she pushed open the door. "Don't worry so much. God will provide a way."

Shelby knew that. In her heart, she knew it, but it was often a lot harder to let go of the worries of tomorrow than it sounded. Were it just her, it would be one thing, but she also carried the worry for the families who needed the center.

Shelby walked across the darkened parking lot and tried not to think about what she would do if the center closed. It had been her job for the last several years - first as a volunteer, then as the manager's assistant, and now as the manager. She couldn't imagine doing anything else.

❧ 14 ❧

T ucker slapped the alarm next to him to shut off
the annoying beeping, but it didn't stop. His
eyes snapped open, and he realized it was not
his alarm going off but his phone. Darkness still lay on the
other side of his windows. What time was it? And who
would be calling him this early?

He grabbed the phone and dread flooded him as he
recognized the number. Why was his sister calling him?
Was she in trouble again? When their mother had died,
Whitley had rebelled, acted out, but he'd thought she had
outgrown most of that behavior.

"Hey, Whitley, what's going on?"

"Tucker, it's Dad. He had a heart attack. You need to
come home." A thread of fear colored her voice. Tucker

wasn't sure he had ever heard her scared, so he knew it must be serious.

"Is he in the hospital?"

"He is. They aren't sure what they are going to do next. They have to run some tests, but they're discussing a quadruple bypass."

A quadruple bypass? Tucker wasn't even sure what that all involved. "How? He eats fairly healthy, doesn't he?"

"They think the stress of work finally got to him. Please tell me you can come home."

Tucker bit the corner of his lip. He was supposed to be at the center in an hour, and he had practice after that. Blaine had told him not to miss any days, but if his dad were really sick that would be an okay reason to, right?

But then he had another shift at the center after practice and dinner with Shelby which he didn't want to miss. "I'll see what I can do, Whitley, but I've got practice and an obligation this evening."

Anger flooded her voice. "What could possibly be more important than seeing your father before he dies?"

"Wait, he's dying?" Even though he and his father hadn't always had the best relationship, he knew that should his father die without Tucker getting to see him that he would regret it for the rest of his life.

"Well, no, but what if he has to have the surgery and dies on the table?"

"You're being dramatic, Whitley, but I'll do my best." He would have to call Coach and clear it with him first. Then he'd have to get ahold of Shelby and make sure she would allow him to make up the work next week. He didn't think it would be an issue, but he had learned assuming wasn't the best option.

He dialed Coach's number first. No doubt the man would not be happy, but Tucker hoped he would grant the time off.

"What's up, Tucker?"

"Hey, Coach, I just received a call from my sister. My dad had a heart attack, and she wants me to see him in case..." He couldn't bring himself to say the words, for fear it would make them come true. "I know it means I'll have to make up some time at the center next week, and it's terrible timing with practice, but is there any way I can take a few days? It's my dad."

Silence echoed from the other end. Coach was probably debating if he were telling the truth or not. "It is a bad time, but family is more important than any game. Go, and I'll tell the team what's happening. Do you think you'll be back for the game?"

The Christmas game was only four days away, but there was no way he was going to miss it. "I'll come back for the game, Coach. I promise."

"All right. Go be with your dad. I'll be praying for him."

The words caught Tucker off guard. For a moment, Coach sounded like his old teammate Emmitt Brown, but Tucker hadn't known Coach was a believer as well. Again, Shelby's words paraded through his mind, reminding him about his own decision to give his anger God; but he pushed them away for the moment. "Thanks, I appreciate it."

"You're welcome. Don't forget to call the woman at the center. You don't want to just not show up for the community service."

"I will." Tucker ended the call and then pulled up a browser window. He didn't have Shelby's number or even the number of the center. Probably, he should have asked for it, but he hadn't thought he would actually have to call her.

The center information appeared on his screen and he clicked on the link to dial the number. Shelby probably wouldn't be there yet, but hopefully they would have voicemail so he could leave a message.

The phone rang four times in his ear. He was about to hang up and try again later when a click finally sounded in his ear. The recording was faint and not very clear, and he wondered if they were using an old answering machine instead of voicemail. He didn't think anyone used them anymore, but the center was so behind the times that it was possible they hadn't joined the rest of the world in that area either.

When he finally heard the beep signaling the end of the announcement, he rambled off his message. "Shelby, it's Tucker. My dad had a heart attack, and I have to return home. I don't know how long I'll be there, but I'll try to be back as soon as I can. I'll make up whatever hours I miss next week and we'll do dinner when I get back. Thanks."

As he hung up the phone, he hoped the message would get to her. She would no doubt be livid if it didn't and she thought he was just ducking the responsibility or standing her up. He'd seen it on her face last night when he'd been late, but he'd done all he could. At least for now.

Shelby glanced at her watch and decided she had time to check the news before heading into work. It wasn't a daily habit, but she did like to know what was going on in the community in case the center needed to help out in any way.

"The Texas Tornadoes have issued a statement that Tucker Jackson will not play on Sunday's game."

Shelby's fork clattered to her plate as her jaw dropped. Not play? Why?

"The decision comes amid charges that Jackson was involved in a bar brawl after the last game. He has been serving community service at the Southlake Community

Center, but evidently that wasn't retribution enough for victim, Jude Renfrow, who came forward last night with the allegations."

Jude Renfrow? So, was that why he had pulled his donation? Had Tucker known? She thought back to the day she'd spoken to Mr. Renfrow. Yes, Tucker had been there, and she'd definitely mentioned Renfrow's name. Yet, Tucker had said nothing. Had he not known the name of the man he fought with? That seemed unlikely. Even if he hadn't known Renfrow, his name would have appeared in the police report unless perhaps the police weren't called. Were police called to bar brawls? Shelby had no idea. She'd never witnessed a bar fight, and she didn't follow police activity on a regular basis.

Then her mind flew to last night. Was that why Tucker had offered to fund the party? Because he knew he'd been the reason her donor pulled? Why wouldn't he just tell her that? Was he ashamed? Or was he playing her? Maybe the dinner invitation had been to butter her up as well, but that made no sense. He wouldn't have known Mr. Renfrow would come forward, would he?

Shelby flicked off the TV and grabbed her coat and purse. She had questions, and she wasn't going to let Tucker off easy. He'd mentioned he had anger issues, but he should have told her about the bar brawl. Especially with the center's reputation at stake.

The parking lot was empty when she arrived, but Tucker had said he'd be in at eight to discuss the Christmas party. It was ten till, giving her just enough time to open the center and rehearse what she was going to say to him.

"Whoa, that is a face that could kill," Kenzi said as she opened the front door. "You better fix that before the kids start showing up or you might scare them away."

Shelby had been expecting Tucker, but he was late. "Did you watch the news this morning?"

A look of incredulousness blanketed Kenzi's face. "You're kidding, right? I never watch the news. It's too depressing. They never talk about the good things, only about all the awful stuff happening in the world, and I don't need to fill my head with that. Why?"

"Turns out Tucker was serving community service for punching a guy in a bar," she said through clenched teeth.

Kenzi's eyes widened to the size of quarters. "What? That's bad, right?"

"Yeah, that's bad. If the parents see this story, they might pull the kids. Even worse? The guy he fought with is Jude Renfrow."

Kenzi's face blanked, and Shelby knew Kenzi was trying to place the name. When her eyes widened, Shelby knew she had figured it out. "Like our donor Jude Renfrow?"

Shelby crossed her arms and nodded. "The very one. No wonder Tucker was willing to fund the party. He has to know he's the reason Mr. Renfrow pulled his donation."

Kenzi's brow furrowed. "But, Tucker is still funding it, right? I mean, the party is still going to happen?"

Shelby shook her head. Kenzi was missing the point. "Well, he said he was going to fund it, but he's not here, and he was supposed to be here ten minutes ago. What if he saw the news and decided he didn't need to fund it anymore since he can't play on Sunday?"

"Wait, what?" Kenzi asked.

Shelby sighed in frustration, but as Kenzi hadn't seen the story, she explained the situation. "The team suspended him for Sunday's game because of Mr. Renfrow's allegation. What if they told him and he decided he didn't need to finish his service? What if he was playing us? Making us think he was having fun, but he was only here because of the requirement?" The thought sobered her. Mostly because she'd thought he'd been connecting with the kids and enjoying himself, but also because of his words last night. If he was pretending to enjoy volunteering, then perhaps he was only pretending to like her. But what could he possibly hope to get from that?

Kenzi rolled her eyes. "You're the sensible one, Shelby, but you're acting crazy right now."

She was, and she knew she was, but what other explanation was there? He hadn't shown up, and he hadn't called. "There's something else I haven't told you, Kenzi. Last night, he asked me to go to dinner with him tonight."

"But that's great. Why do you look like that's not great?"

"Because he's not here." Shelby threw her hands up in frustration. "What if he was playing me too?"

Kenzi crossed the room to Shelby and picked up her hand. "I think you know that isn't true. Now, I don't know why Tucker hasn't called, but maybe he's stuck in traffic. Or maybe he overslept. He was probably tired after last night. Have you tried calling him?"

"Of course I tried calling him, but I just got his voicemail."

"Then you keep trying. I don't know what happened in the bar fight, but you should hear his side of the story before you jump to any conclusions. You owe him that much."

Kenzi was right. Shelby knew that what was on TV was usually only half of the story, and Tucker hadn't given her a reason to doubt him. Other than his not being here right now. The phone rang beside her, and Shelby picked it up. "Southlake Community Center, how can I help you?"

"Is this Shelby Doll?"

"Yes, may I ask who this is?"

"This is Melissa Utting. I'm Colson's mother."

Shelby's heart sank. Had Colson said something about Tucker's intervention last night? "Yes, Mrs. Utting, how can I help you?"

"I'm calling about the story I saw on the news this morning." Shelby forced herself to remain calm and collected, but this was exactly what she'd been afraid of. "Why on earth do you have someone who was charged with assault working with the kids there?"

Assault? The story she had watched had said nothing about assault charges. Had there been something more or had Melissa read more into the story than what was said. "I understand your concern, Melissa. However, I am unaware of any assault charge."

Melissa cut her off, and the anger in her voice could have started a fire. "Did you watch the news this morning?"

"I did. I saw that Tucker has been suspended due to allegations, but there was no mention of an assault charge. Besides, we are a center that allows people to serve community service here. I am not sure of the circumstances behind the allegations, but I can tell you that Tucker has been great with the kids."

"Well, Colson will not be returning. Any center that would allow an athlete to work there who probably bought his way out of an assault charge is not some place I want my son."

Shelby was about to respond when the loud click

followed by the dial tone told her that Melissa was no longer on the other end. While she didn't feel Melissa pulling Colson was that big of a loss, especially after the bullying incident, she feared that this phone call was going to be the first of many.

15

Tucker stared at the looming hospital in front of him and swallowed his discomfort. Even though his mother had died at home and not in a hospital, he still equated the sterile buildings with her death. Maybe it was the smell of antiseptic that coated the halls, the same smell that masked his mother's scent after she was gone. Or maybe the pale cream walls themselves were to blame. They were the same pale cream color that reminded him of the sheet they pulled over her face before taking her away. Whatever it was, he hated hospitals. Hated the sight, the sound, and the smell of them; yet here he was being forced to enter one again.

His foot took a step as if it remembered how to walk even while his brain didn't, but it was a slow and halting step. He probably looked as if he was the injured one in need of a hospital as he crossed the parking lot instead of his father. His father. The man who hadn't been there for Tucker or Whitley since he wife died, so why was Tucker here for him now? Because he felt obligated to? Because he was family? Or was it because of the frailty of life? Perhaps it was a combination of all three. It was one thing to be angry at his father, to allow that to keep him from coming home more often; but it was another thing entirely to not see him knowing he could be on his deathbed.

Heart surgeries were more common now than they once were; and after searching quadruple bypasses, he knew that most ended well. But it was the ones that didn't end well that sat with him. Any surgery had a risk of complication, but he imagined the risks were higher when your chest was cracked open, and someone messed around with your heart.

Somehow he made it across the parking lot and through the main doors. A stop at the reception desk earned him a visitor pass and directions to room 312. And then he was in the elevator. As the doors closed, he felt as if they were closing off his air supply as well. His hand pulled at his collar as if the few inches of give would allow him to breathe easier. Black spots darted across his vision, and his hand found the wall as a wave of dizziness swept over him. Then the elevator chimed, and the doors slid open.

The black dots receded, but the pressure did not. Still,

he managed to step over the line, allowing the doors to close behind him. The dim hum of conversations and computers floated on the air, sounding muted in his brain. His eyes found the small gray plaque indicating room 312 lay to the left, and he forced his feet that direction.

The door to room 312 lay ajar, and he paused to take one final deep breath before pushing the door open. His father appeared still and quiet in the bed, and Whitley sat in a chair nearby with a book on her lap. Her gaze lifted at the sound of Tucker's footsteps, and her eyes widened.

"Tucker, you made it," she said as she launched herself out of the chair and across the room.

She was thinner than he remembered, but her smile appeared the same. Bright and wide, it showed off her dimple and dispelled all the shadows that had been hanging over his head. "I told you I would try, Whit."

Her arms wound around his neck and squeezed as if she was afraid he might be an apparition and disappear if she wasn't holding onto him. "I know, but I didn't think you'd actually show up."

Guilt pulled at his heart. It had been too long. He should have come home, even if it was just to see her.

"Tucker?" His father's voice was quiet and scratchy and it ended the brother-sister reunion.

Reluctantly, he stepped toward the bed. "I'm here, Dad."

"I told her not to call you. I know how busy you are with football and the incident."

"It was dropped, Dad. The team gave me community service for it, but it's okay. Thank you." The words reminded him that his father had been too busy to show up and bail him out in the first place.

"I'm sorry I didn't go. Big case."

"There's always a big case, Dad." Tucker didn't mean for the words to be hurtful, but he saw the emotion flash in his father's eyes nonetheless. "I'm used to you not showing up by now."

"Tucker." Whitley hissed in a shocked voice, but their father held up his hand.

"No, he's right, Whitley. I haven't been there for him, for either of you. I've been so consumed with my own grief that I didn't realize you two must have been grieving as well."

The conversation with Benji played again in Tucker's head. He'd figured out that night that his father hadn't hated him, but he hadn't realized how much he needed to hear the words until now. Was this what Shelby had meant when she'd discussed forgiving his father? Was this God at work? Shelby. She still hadn't returned his call. He hoped she wasn't too angry with him.

Before he could say anything, his phone vibrated in his pocket. He pulled it out expecting it to be Shelby, but the number wasn't the one he had called previously. "I'll be right back." Tucker wasn't sure why he felt the need to explain his actions. He was a grown man, and he could take a phone call if he needed to.

"Hello?" he asked when he crossed the doorway and entered the hall.

"Tucker, it's Coach."

Dread filled Tucker, coursing like poison through every vein. Coach never called unless there was trouble, and he'd cleared the leave with him this morning. "Hey, Coach. What can I do for you?"

The man exhaled a large sigh. "It's about Sunday, Tucker. The man involved with the altercation called the league."

"What?" Anger and frustration erupted within Tucker, fighting for control. "Can he do that? I was never charged."

"I know, but you know how image is. It's everything; and so, even though the league knows you weren't at fault, they want to send a message. They're suspending you for Sunday's game."

"No, they can't do that. It's the playoffs, Coach. The next game is the wild card game. If we lose, we're out. I can't not play on the possible last game of the season." Frustration edged ahead of anger, and Tucker ran his hand across the back of his neck, massaging the muscles that now stood rigid with tension.

"I know it's the playoffs, Tucker, but I can't get you out

of this one. It's just one game. If we win it, you'll still be able to play in the quarter finals, the semi finals, and the championship game."

"Is there anything I can do?" Tucker asked. This was a nightmare. He'd worked so hard the last few days. And he'd changed. He could feel it.

"I doubt it, but you could try doing something to improve your image. Issue a public apology, help out a charity, something to show them that's not the real you."

Images of the center and it's used equipment flashed into Tucker's mind. He'd brought some footballs already, but what if he supplied a whole new collection of sports equipment? What if he did it at the Christmas party? In fact, what if he got some of the other guys to go with him to the party? It could be a big team event and maybe even boost morale before the big game.

"Still no word from him?" Kenzi asked as Shelby massaged her temples.

"None, and I just keep getting his voicemail. I don't know why he wouldn't at least call and explain. Now, it appears he might not be funding the party after all, and I have no one else to call and no money to buy gifts for the kids." She lifted her eyes to Kenzi's and sighed.

"Okay, that does stink," Kenzi said. True to her

personality, Kenzi was still trying to find the silver lining in the dark clouds that filled Shelby's vision. "Maybe we can find some leftover things around here?"

"That's all we have is leftover things, Kenzi. Leftover things that nobody wants." The ringing of the phone interrupted her pity party, and Shelby forced a smile she didn't feel to her face as she picked up the phone. "Southlake Community Center, this is Shelby, how may I help you?"

"Shelby, thank goodness. Did you get my message?"

Tucker's voice both irritated her and sent her heart fluttering. Ugh, why did he affect her so much? "No, I saw no message, and I've been trying to call you for hours. Where are you Tucker? You're supposed to be here helping plan the Christmas party for tomorrow night."

"I know, but my dad had a heart attack. I had to fly to San Antonio to see him and I just got your messages, but I want you to still go ahead with the party for tomorrow."

"Tucker, are you sure? The news-"

"I don't care about the news, Shelby. I should have told you sooner about Jude Renfrow, and I'm sorry. But he's not important now. What's important is making sure those kids have a Christmas."

Was she dreaming? She pinched her arm to make sure she was really awake. Tucker Jackson didn't care about the suspension and he still wanted to fund the party? She could barely believe it, but though she appreciated his selflessness, it still didn't answer the bigger problem. "How? I have no money, no decorations, nothing."

"I'm going to wire you some money. Use it to get whatever decorations you need. Also, call the media and see if you can get Sylvie Sanders back out. I'll cover the gifts, and I promise I'll be back tomorrow for the party."

"But your dad?"

"I'll figure it out. You take care of things on your end, and I'll take care of things on mine. Seven o'clock tomorrow, we'll show those kids a party they won't soon forget."

"Okay, if you say so." She hung up the phone and turned to Kenzi, still dazed at what had just transpired.

"Was that Tucker?"

"It was. He said he left a message about today. Evidently his father had a heart attack."

Kenzi's hand flew to her mouth. "Oh my gosh, is he okay?"

"I don't know. I forgot to ask." Shelby couldn't believe she had forgotten that simple courtesy. She definitely had too much on her mind right now. "Anyway, he said he was wiring money and that I was to take care of the decorations and spreading the word. He said he'd take care of the gifts."

"Well, we better get started then. We've got a lot to do before tomorrow night."

16

"So, has a doctor told you anything?" Tucker asked when he returned to the room. He suddenly had a lot on his plate that he needed to do.

"The doctor was in this morning before you got here. They think they can insert a stent. Why? Are you in a hurry to run off somewhere?" Whitley crossed her arms and arched her left eyebrow as if she thought she could intimidate Tucker with her expression.

"That call was my coach. The guy who punched me contacted the league and they want to suspend me for Sunday's game."

"Can they do that?" his father asked. "I thought I got the charges dropped."

"You did, but evidently they want to make a lesson out of

this. However, that's water under the bridge. The bigger issue is this center where I've been volunteering. I was supposed to be there today to help fund and plan a Christmas party for the kids, and these kids deserve a party. Some of them have very little. So, I need to make some calls; and I'll have to fly back tomorrow, but I want to be here for the surgery if I can."

His father's eyes glistened with unshed tears, and he blinked them away then coughed to clear his throat. "I think that's a great idea, Tucker, and even if it means you have to miss my surgery, it's okay with me."

Whitley stood and placed her hand on his forehead. "Are you sure you're feeling okay? You're willing to spend money to throw a party for other people even though it might not help you out? Who are you and what have you done with my big brother?"

"Hey, I help people," he said, but as the words left his mouth, he realized Whitley was right. He had been selfish. He'd been thinking about how the losses affected him and not about the rest of the men on the team. He'd been wallowing in his sorrows which caused him to be in the wrong place at the wrong time. And he'd dismissed community service at first because it would take up his time.

"Okay, maybe you're right. I haven't been the best example of helping people, but working at the center has made me see things differently."

"Well, I'm proud of you," Whitley said squeezing his shoulder.

"Me too," his father said from the bed. "What can we do to help?"

"I want to purchase new equipment for the center and then I need someone to go shopping for toys for the kids."

Whitley tossed her hair over her shoulders and placed her hands on her hips. "I'm a great shopper. I could run and get toys."

"Awesome." He pulled his wallet out of his pocket and handed her a credit card. "Take this and buy at least fifty gifts."

Her eyes widened. "Fifty? Do I have a limit?"

Tucker chuckled. "Well, try not to break the bank but no, no limit."

"This is going to be so much fun." As the light glistened in her eyes, he wondered if he had just made a terrible mistake.

"Dad, do you think you feel up to shopping online for some equipment for the center? I need basketballs, softballs, jump ropes, the like."

"I can do that," his father said. "Scrolling and clicking is my specialty."

"Great." Tucker handed the laptop to his father. "No work, just shopping."

His father rolled his eyes but promised. Tucker took out his phone and sat down in one of the nearby chairs.

He had a lot of phone calls to make, but before he dialed the first number, his eyes wandered to his father. Could this be the start of a better relationship for them? If so, he knew he had two people he needed to thank - Shelby and God.

"Yes, that's right. Tomorrow night at seven p.m. It's going to be an amazing community event and Tucker Jackson asked specifically for Sylvie Sanders. Can she make it?" Shelby swallowed the seed of jealousy that had sprouted in her stomach when Tucker requested Sylvie. She knew it was probably just because the woman had already covered one story and would be the natural choice to do the next one as well; but as she still wasn't sure where she stood with Tucker. He hadn't mentioned rescheduling their date when he'd called.

"I think we can make that work. I'll put the story on Sylvie's docket."

"Thank you so much." Shelby hung up the phone and shook her head. She'd spent the last week worrying that this event would never happen, but now it appeared unstoppable. She and Kenzi had picked up the money from Tucker and purchased Christmas decorations and food. Then Kenzi had begun decorating while Shelby called to get the media coverage in place. The newspaper and the local news and radio stations had agreed to send someone out, and Shelby had a feeling this would be their best Christmas party ever.

A giant smile parted Shelby's lips as she exited the reception area to see the kids helping Kenzi decorate. Jingle Bells played softly on an old boombox, but the kids didn't seem to care. They were laughing and smiling in a way that Shelby hadn't seen in a long time. Darby was standing on a chair helping Kenzi hang streamers while Benji sorted out the strings of Christmas lights. Quinn and Kayla were setting up the artificial tree while still others were pulling the freshly purchased ornaments out of the box.

"How can I help?" Shelby asked as she neared the group. "We have to get this place ready for tomorrow night."

"Is Mr. Tucker coming to help too?" Benji asked.

"He had to go see his dad, but he's helping from down there, and he promised he'll be back tomorrow for the party," Shelby said.

"We should do something special for him for hosting the thing last night," Darby said as she pushed her glasses up her nose. "That was really nice of him to show us how to play even though I don't really like football."

Shelby smiled at the girl. "You're right. It was. We should do something nice for him. Do you guys have any ideas?"

"We could make him a card," Darby said. "Something colorful and pretty and maybe with unicorns on it."

Shelby mashed her lips together to keep from laughing. Somehow she doubted Tucker was the unicorn kind. "I think that would be lovely, but maybe something else as well since he's a boy and probably more of a sports fan than a unicorn fan."

"We could give him a football," Quinn said, "though I'm not sure he would want any of ours."

"Do we have enough to purchase a new football, Ms. Shelby?" Benji asked pausing his untangling to shoot her a very serious look.

"I think we might. What are you thinking?"

"What if we got him a new football and we all signed it. You know like people do with a cast. Only he wouldn't have to cut it off and he could keep it forever."

Shelby swallowed the emotion rising in her throat and forced her hand to stay at her side and not dab at her eyes. She knew if she did, the flood gate would drop and she would end up crying in front of the kids which would probably scare them more than anything. "That's a great idea, Benji."

"Yeah, great idea, man," Quinn said as he clapped a hand on Benji's shoulder.

The other kids echoed their agreement, and Shelby watched Benji sit just a little taller in his chair. Yes. This. This was exactly what had been missing before Tucker came into their lives. "Well, I guess I better run to the store and grab a football then so you guys have a chance to sign it tonight. Can you hold down the fort for a bit, Kenzi?"

"Are you kidding? I'm totally in my element here."

It was true. Kenzi looked like a natural as she hung the streamers, and as Shelby looked around, she realized the gym had already been transformed into something magical. Perhaps Kenzi had found her calling after all.

17

"Where is he?" Shelby asked, wringing her hands for the fifth time in fewer than five minutes as she checked the front door again. It was six thirty, and they would be opening the doors soon, but Tucker was nowhere to be seen.

Kenzi placed a hand on her arm. "Relax. He'll be here."

"What if he doesn't show up? He hasn't even called today. What if he got in a wreck or something happened to his dad? We have no presents if he doesn't show up."

Kenzi grabbed both of Shelby's shoulders and shook her. "Stop it. You'll drive yourself crazy with what ifs. What is it you always say about worry?"

Shelby sighed as she pictured the pastor at her church

sharing the wisdom that had stuck with her for so many years. "Worrying accomplishes nothing except taking time away from today." She knew the pastor was right, and the Bible mentioned often not to worry but cast those fears on Jesus instead, but it was a lot easier said than done.

"Right. This is going to be a magical evening, Shelby. Don't tarnish it by worrying about what you can't control."

Shelby took a deep breath and nodded. The place was magical. Kenzi had hung twinkly lights around the room along with wreaths and streamers in red, green, and white. The artificial tree, while small, twinkled merrily and boasted the many ornaments the kids had hung on it. It even had a few uneven strands of popcorn though none long enough to wrap all the way around as the kids had eaten it before it reached that point. A long table held the cookies and treats Shelby had picked up on the way here as well as punch and cups, plates, and napkins. All that was missing were the kids, who were on their way, and the presents.

Shelby glanced out the window again and ran a hand down her red party dress. She almost never wore red, but Kenzi had been adamant that she wear something bright and festive tonight. Kenzi had also done her makeup even though Shelby had protested the red lip color that matched her dress but seemed too bright for her. Without a conscious thought, her hand found the tendril that never stayed up with the rest of her hair, and she tugged on it.

"Will you stop?" Kenzi scolded, slapping her hand down.

Shelby flushed. She hated getting caught twirling that hair, but she supposed she could have worse habits. In high school, she had known a girl who pulled out her eyebrows and eyelashes. Often times, she would come to school with entire patches missing. There was also a boy who had scratched at his arm so often that it would bleed. The teacher would stop the bleeding, the wound would scab over, and then he would scratch the scab off and make it bleed again. Yes, in comparison, her hair twirling was a minor, albeit obnoxious, habit.

Headlights flashed, blinding her, as a car pulled into the parking lot. *Please be him*, she thought. *Please be Tucker.*

But it wasn't. She recognized Benji's mother's car as soon as it grew closer. "Do we let them in?" she asked Kenzi in a quiet voice.

"Of course we do," Kenzi said. "It's freezing out there, and I promise everything will be okay."

Shelby nodded, but as another car pulled in, she couldn't help but wonder what they would do if Tucker didn't show.

❄

"Thanks for agreeing to this guys." Tucker looked around at the assembled group of football players. Not only had most of the guys from his team agreed to come; but Emmitt, his old teammate from the Rebels, had arrived as well. The Rebels were already out of the playoffs for the year, and as his wife's family lived close to Southlake, he decided he would help out and then drive out to meet them.

"What exactly are we doing, Tucker?" Emmitt asked.

"We are playing Santa to some kids who deserve it," Tucker said with a smile. He had spent entirely too much money on the toys and new equipment, but he knew in his heart it would be worth it. "So grab a gift and let's load up."

He glanced at his watch as the guys began grabbing packages. They were a little behind schedule, but he didn't think Shelby would mind when she saw what he had in store. He grabbed a few packages and carried them out to his truck. The back was already loaded up with presents, but there was room for two more. He slid them in and then turned to see how the other guys were doing. They had decided to ride three in a truck, but even with that, they needed four trucks to bring all the packages.

When the last box was loaded and the men were situated in the trucks, Tucker climbed behind the wheel of his own. Emmitt and Blaine were riding with him, something he never thought he'd see.

"This is a nice gesture," Emmitt said as Tucker turned the key.

"Thanks, Rev. I guess you rubbed off on me more than you or I knew."

Blaine, surprisingly, stayed quiet, but Tucker didn't mind. He enjoyed catching up with Emmitt as they drove to the center.

His eyes widened as he pulled into the center's parking lot though. There were more cars than he could remember seeing parked in the parking lot. So many that he was forced to park in the fire lane because there were no open spots.

"Are all these cars here for the party?" Blaine asked.

"I think so," Tucker said.

"I hope we brought enough gifts," Emmitt said as if reading Tucker's mind.

"Well, if we didn't, then I'll just have to go shopping again tomorrow."

As he turned the engine off, he spied a figure clad in red speeding in his direction. Was that Shelby? He blinked, not believing his eyes. He'd assumed from the color of the dress that it had to be Kenzi, but Kenzi's hair was dark; and the hair on this woman was definitely blonde. His heart skipped a beat as he stepped out to meet her.

"What took you so long?" she asked when she was

within earshot. "The kids are waiting inside and I'm running out of ways to entertain them."

He could hear the frustration in her voice, and it matched the expression on her face. But he couldn't concentrate on her words. His focus was drawn to her mouth. Her beautiful lips were painted cherry red, and they screamed that they wanted to be kissed. There was makeup around her eyes that brought out their color as well, and something about the red against her skin made it appear creamier than he remembered. Every bone in his body ached to take her in his arms, but he couldn't do that right now. Right now was about the kids.

"I'm sorry." He took her hands, unable to keep himself from touching a small part of her. "We took a little longer loading up than I thought we would, but I promise it will be worth it."

She glanced briefly down at their hands before meeting his gaze. "We?"

At that moment, the passenger door opened behind him and Blaine and Emmitt stepped out. Then, as if in sync, the door of the other three trucks opened and their players tumbled out as well.

"Yeah. We. I brought a few friends." He squeezed her hands, enjoying the expression of shock painted across her face. "Now go tell those kids that it's time to open presents."

With a final incredulous glance, she turned around and dashed back into the center. Tucker turned to his friends and motioned them with his hands. "Let's go, boys."

Tucker could scarcely believe it was the same center as he walked in. The feel of Christmas was everywhere - from the decorative wreaths hung about the room to the sounds of White Christmas playing softly over the speakers to the artificial Christmas tree near the far end. It sparkled with every color of light and probably every ornament the center had from the looks of it. The only thing it was missing was presents.

The room had been filled with a dull chatter, but as he and the other football players walked in, a hush fell across the room. Kids and parents alike stared at them as if the men were mirages in a desert, and everyone appeared afraid to make the first move or say a word for fear they might disappear.

"It's Tucker." Benji's voice echoed across the room, and Tucker smiled. He was glad Benji was here. He had a special present for the boy. "I knew he'd make it."

And then the dam broke. The kids raced across the floor shouting "Merry Christmas" and asking "Is that for me?"

"One at a time," Tucker said with a smile. "Let my friends set the gifts down first." The children quieted, but

Tucker could see their contained energy with each bounce of a foot or bob of a head. They were calm but it wouldn't last long. "First, let me introduce my friends. This is my friend Emmitt Brown. I played with him on the San Antonio Rebels where he still plays. He drove down just to meet you guys."

Eyes widened and jaws dropped as the kids looked at Emmitt. "Next to him is Blaine Hollis. I'm sure you guys recognize him as the quarterback for the Tornadoes." He continued the process until every player had been introduced. "Now, my friends have some gifts for you guys. Who wants presents?"

The screams of the children rocked Tucker back, and he chuckled. They were certainly excited. "All right, let's open some presents. If you like dolls and dress-up clothes, I want you to find a player holding a pink gift, and if you like sports and cars, find a player with a blue gift."

As they hadn't known who all would be in attendance or what they might like, Tucker had figured wrapping them pink and blue would be easier. This would allow the kids to choose the type of gift they might enjoy more. The children scrambled around deciding on which gift they wanted, and when every child had one, Tucker gave the announcement they could open them.

Chaos ensued. Paper was ripped and thrown into the air. Squeals of laughter and shouts of joy echoed throughout the room; and as soon as their gift was open, the kids were off showing it to their parents, their friends, or just playing with it in the middle of the floor.

Tucker touched the gifts still in his pocket as he made his way over to Benji and his mother. Benji had ended up with a microscope, something Tucker was sure the boy would enjoy with his love of science. "Hey Benji, do you like your gift?"

The smile on the boy's face said more than words ever could. "I love it, Mr. Tucker. Thanks for doing this for us."

His mother - a pale, frail woman with mousy brown hair who looked as if life had been harder on her than necessary - sniffed and wiped a tear from her eye. "Yes, thank you. This is more than we could have hoped for."

Emotion choked Tucker's throat, and he coughed to clear it. "I actually have one more gift for Benji if that's okay?"

Questions filled her eyes, but she nodded.

"Benji, I probably won't be playing in the game, but I have two tickets with your name on them. Would you like to come see the Tornadoes play in person? You and your mother would be my guests in the luxury box."

Benji's eyes grew to the size of half dollars. "Really? Me?"

"Yes, you." Tucker knelt in front of the boy and placed a hand on his knee. "I don't have any kids yet, but when I do, I hope I have a son just like you, so it would be amazing if you could come to the game."

Benji turned his face to his mother. "Mom, can we?"

"It's too much." Emotion filled her voice and another tear escaped from her eye.

"No, it's not. Please, come." He placed the two tickets in her hand. "I insist. Merry Christmas."

She nodded and though she could say no more, he could read the thanks in her teary gaze.

"That was very kind of you, Tucker."

Tucker turned to see Sylvie Sanders and her cameraman behind him. "Thank you. I'm glad you could make it. Have you had a chance to get some footage of the party?"

"I have, but I am curious as to why you called me out here. Does this have anything to do with your suspension for Sunday's game?"

So, she'd heard about that. He opened his mouth to tell her it did. To tell her that Jude Renfrow had been the donor last year and pulled his donation because of the skirmish with Tucker, but then he realized his motives for donating to this party would come into questions. Yes, he wanted to play Sunday, more than anything; but he didn't want to ruin this moment for the kids.

"It actually isn't, Sylvie. I called you out here because I wanted the people of Southlake to see what an amazing center this is, what fantastic kids these are, and what an outstanding job Director Shelby Doll is doing here. This party almost didn't happen because they couldn't find a donor to fund it. I couldn't let that happen. After volunteering here for the last week, I have seen first hand how important this center is to the families who use it. I know not everyone can donate the way I did, but everyone can do something even if it's volunteering."

"So, you don't care about the game Sunday?"

Tucker smiled and shook his head. "Of course I care about the game Sunday. It's the wild card game. If we win, we continue on in the playoffs, but if we lose it will be the last game of the season. Do I wish I was playing? Absolutely. But I learned an important lesson. I was suspended because I got into an altercation with someone after our last game. Even though I didn't throw the first punch and was just defending myself, I was in the bar because I was angry. I was angry at our loss, angry at being traded, angry at my father; but working here let me see how misplaced that anger was. It showed me how lucky I am to play on a great team with other amazing players who came out tonight to help me bring some Christmas cheer to these kids."

"Well, that is certainly a feel good story that our viewers will enjoy," Sylvie said as she motioned for the cameraman to stop rolling. "Off the record though, do you know why the previous donor chose not to donate this year?"

Tucker flashed her a tight-lipped smile. He knew what she was trying to do, but he wasn't going to bite. He'd given her enough information that if she really wanted to run with that story, she could look it up herself. Instead, he pointed over her shoulder at the refreshment table. "I need to see Shelby about something. If you'll excuse me."

18

"This is amazing, Tucker. I can't believe you pulled all this together in just a day," Shelby said as he approached her. She held out a glass of punch to him and then filled a second cup for herself.

"You did all the hard work, Shelby. I just got the toys here." He took a sip of the punch, but his eyes never left her face.

Shelby's heart quickened in her chest. The way he was looking at her felt like a caress. She could almost feel his hand against her cheek, and the thought of it sent her blood pulsing through her body. "You did a lot more than that, Tucker Jackson. Don't think I don't know it."

"Well, I have two more things for you. Will you follow me?"

Follow him? With the way he was looking at her right

now? She'd probably follow him off a cliff right now if he asked. "Sure." The word barely made it past her throat and came out more like a whisper than an answer, but he seemed to understand it anyway.

He took her cup and placed it on the table along with his own. Then he reached for her hand. Warm tingles shot up her arm as their skin touched, and Shelby fought to compose her breathing. He led her toward the door. "Wait, my coat."

"Don't worry about it. You can use my jacket. We won't be long." He paused long enough to shrug out of his suit jacket and place it on her shoulders.

She knew the chill was biting outside, but even when they stepped out of the warmth of the center, she didn't feel it. It was as if their connection was heating them both.

"I got a few more things for the center," he said as he steered them toward the back of his truck.

Her eyes widened as she saw the new sports equipment in the bed of the truck. "Tucker, you didn't have to do this."

"Yes, I did. Have you tried playing basketball with those balls?"

She chuckled at the seriousness in his voice and shook her head. "I know how awful they are. I don't play, but I've watched the kids try to use them. Still, this is too much. You've done so much already."

"If I plan to keep volunteering, I'd like to have better equipment."

Her lips parted and she stared up at him. "Do you mean it? You want to keep volunteering?" She had hoped he would want to stay, but she hadn't wanted to ask him for fear of his answer.

He took her other hand and pulled her close to his chest. "If you'll let me."

Suddenly, it was harder to breathe. It was as if a hand was squeezing her lungs closed. "Of course I'll let you."

The corners of his lips twitched, showing off the dimple in his cheek. "Good, there's just one more thing then."

"What's that?" Shelby could hardly get the words out. She felt locked in his gaze. The smell of him intoxicated her - this manly scent that reminded her of campfires and woods. It made her want to close her eyes and breathe in deeply.

"We need to get you to relax a little." He let go of one of her hands, and she watched in slow motion as his hand touched her hair. With deft fingers, he pulled the first pin out, and she felt a chunk of hair fall and bounce by her face. Then another pin and finally the clip holding it all in place.

She wanted to say something, to do something, though she had no idea what. But she couldn't. Her feet were frozen in place. Her eyes were locked with his. It was taking all her effort just to remember to breathe. And then his hand was in her hair, and the feel of it sent the tiny hairs on the back of her neck up. Goosebumps broke out on her arms, and she closed her eyes, relishing the sensation.

"That's better." His hand moved from her hair to the back of her neck, and Shelby's eyes snapped open. Was he going to kiss her? She could see the desire in his eyes, hear it in the thudding of his heart. Or was that hers? It appeared she could no longer tell the difference.

"I have one more question for you, Shelby Doll." His voice was husky and constricted with emotion.

"Yes?" The word was airy, far off, as if she had answered from another plane.

"Would it be breaking any rules if I kissed the director of the center?" The twinkling in his eye told her he didn't really care if it did. He was going to kiss her unless she protested, and she had no plans to do that.

She managed a small shake of her head, and then warmth flooded her body as his lips touched hers. Having always been the shy, quiet one, Shelby hadn't kissed that many men; but she didn't think she would ever forget this kiss with Tucker. Electricity buzzed through her, racing down her legs and curling her toes in her shoes.

"Oh, I do have one more gift for you," Tucker said when they pulled back.

Shelby couldn't imagine what else he might have for

her. He'd already given her more than she expected. "What is it?"

"I probably won't get to play because of this suspension, but will you be my guest at the game on Christmas?" He pulled out two tickets from his pocket. "There's one for Kenzi too."

"Of course, I'd be happy to, but there has to be something we can do so you can play." She couldn't stand the thought of him not getting to do the thing he loved the most. He had changed so much. The man who stood before her today was no longer the angry man who had entered her center a week ago.

He brushed her hair behind her ear and shook his head. "No, but it's fine. It's just a game. Working with you and with these kids the last week has shown me that."

Shelby could tell it was still more than a game to him, but he was trying to accept it. She had to try and help him.

Tucker could tell from the glint in her eye that Shelby wasn't going to just let it go, but at least she didn't push him for more information.

"Okay, if you're sure."

"I am." She shivered in his arms, and the reality of the

cold air around them landed on his shoulders. "We should get back inside. You're freezing."

"I'm fine," she said through chattering teeth. "How's your dad?"

"He's good. They put the stent in yesterday afternoon. He has to stay another day for observation, but then he should be able to return home. I, uh, took your advice too, on the way back here. I opened my heart to God. He's helping me forgive my father and myself."

Tears clouded Shelby's eyes, and she blinked them back. "That's wonderful, Tucker. Oh, and I almost forgot. The kids have something for you too."

"For me?" He couldn't imagine what the kids might have for him, but he followed Shelby back into the center.

"There you two are," Kenzi said, hurrying up to them. "The kids have been asking for you. They want to give Tucker his gift."

"Let's not make them wait any longer," Shelby said with a smile. She led Tucker to the middle of the room and held up her hands to get the attention of the crowd. "Thank you all for coming out. I especially want to thank Tucker Jackson and the rest of the Texas Tornadoes for helping out. I know the kids have enjoyed having you here the last week; and as a way of saying thank you, they have a gift for you."

Tucker watched as Benji rolled his direction with a

colorfully wrapped package on his lap. "I hope you like it, Mr. Tucker."

"I'm sure I'll love it," Tucker said as he took the box. He shot the crowd a teasing grin. "Should I open it now?"

"Open it," the kids hollered back at him.

"Okay, okay." He tore the paper and lifted the lid to see a football inside. "Ah, you guys, this is great."

"It's not just a football, Mr. Tucker," Benji said with a shake of his head. "Take it out."

Tucker did as instructed, and his throat swelled with emotion as he pulled out the football covered in kids' scribbles. They had all signed the football and some had even left him a note or encouraging word. "This is perfect, guys. Thank you."

And it was. Tucker knew even if they made it to the championship game that this would be the highlight of his season.

🕸 19 🕸

The ringing of his phone woke Tucker on Christmas morning. Was it his father? Whitley? She'd promised to call when his father got released. His hand grabbed the phone, and he hit the answer call button without looking at the caller ID.

"Hello?"

"Tucker? It's Coach. You ready to suit up today?"

"Suit up? But I thought I was suspended."

"You were, but your teammates called the league last night and said they weren't playing without you. Then the league received a second call informing them of Mr. Renfrow's decision to pull his donation to the community center. In light of those two things, they have lifted your suspension."

His teammates refused to play without him? He could

barely believe it. Here he'd thought he wasn't fitting in on this team, yet they had shown up to help him out last night and then stood up to the league for him. He couldn't have asked for better team members. "Thanks, Coach. I'll be there." Tucker couldn't help smiling as he hung up the phone and headed into the shower. This Christmas was already shaping up to be his best since his mother passed away, and getting to play was icing on the cake.

Two hours later, he pulled into the stadium parking lot. He'd told Shelby and Benji's mother where to go, but he hoped he would get to see them before the game started. Tucker saw his favorite guard Dennis on duty; and he made his way over to him.

"Merry Christmas, Dennis, how's the family?"

"A little irritated I'm here on Christmas Day," Dennis said, "but they're good."

Tucker had never considered all the people who also had to give up Christmas with their families to be here. "I'm sorry you have to be away from your family on Christmas. I'll tell you what, next year I'll save Christmas Day tickets for you. That way your family can watch from the luxury box. They still won't get to spend the day with you directly, but at least you'll be in the same place."

Dennis's eyes widened. "You would do that?"

"Of course I would. I'd give you some for today, but I already gave them out which reminds me of why I came over here. If a boy in a wheelchair and a beautiful blonde come through here with my luxury box tickets, will you tell them I'll come see them before the game starts if I can?"

"You bet Mr. Jackson. I'll keep my eyes open for them."

"Thanks, Dennis. Again, Merry Christmas."

"Merry Christmas to you Mr. Jackson and good luck today."

Tucker flashed another warm smile before he continued into the dressing room. Somehow, he didn't think they would need good luck today. Everything about it just felt right.

"Oh my goodness," Kenzi said as she entered the luxury box behind Shelby. "This is amazing."

"This is insane," Shelby said as she took in the luxurious gold and blue interior. "Who needs this much?"

Kenzi shook her head and rolled her eyes. "Nobody needs it. That's why it's called a luxury, but isn't it fantastic?" She held her arms wide and fell into a plush leather couch.

Shelby didn't know if fantastic was the word she would use. She felt like an imposter in the exorbitant room, and she couldn't help thinking about all the kids she could help if she had this kind of money.

"I know what you're thinking, Shelby, but can't you

just relax for one day? Can't you just take a step back and enjoy this for what it is? A treat. An inside look into how the other half lives."

"You're right," Shelby said with a sigh. "It's Christmas, and I should enjoy this. I'll probably never do this again."

Kenzi snorted and sat up. "Who are you kidding? I saw the way Tucker was looking at you last night. I have a feeling you'll be attending a lot of these in the future."

Heat flamed up Shelby's face. Kenzi didn't even know about the kiss. Shelby normally told her everything, but she couldn't tell her about the kiss with Tucker. It had just been too mind blowing.

"Whoa, look at this place." Benji's voice gave Shelby a reprieve from answering Kenzi, one she was very grateful for.

"Hey Benji. Pretty cool, right?" Shelby had been thrilled when Tucker told her he had given a ticket to Benji and his mother, but seeing the awed expression on his face was even more heartwarming. Maybe if she did continue dating Tucker, they could bring a different kid each week. That might be the only way she wouldn't feel so bad about watching the game from this box.

"Oh good, you both made it."

Shelby turned at the sound of Tucker's voice. She'd never seen him up close in his football gear, and it took her breath away. He'd always been just Tucker to her, but in his tight pants and jersey, he looked like a football player. "Thank you for inviting us."

"Thank you for coming."

He didn't cross the room and take her in his arms as she'd hoped he would, but his gaze said it all. It was as if time slowed around them, and every sound was muted. She could read the desire in his gaze, and the heat returned when she realized everyone else probably could too.

"Mr. Tucker, this is so cool." Once again, Benji came to her aid even though he had no idea he was doing it.

"I'm glad you're enjoying it," Tucker said with a chuckle. "I have to get down for the warmup, but I wanted to say hi before I did." His eyes shifted back to Shelby. "Will you wait for me after?"

"Of course." There was no way Shelby would leave without seeing him. It was Christmas Day and though she didn't get to spend the day close to him, she had hopes they would spend at least a little of the evening together. She watched him wave and exit the room before going to sit on the couch next to Kenzi.

"See, I told you," Kenzi whispered as Shelby sat down.

"Yes, you're very smart. Now hush so I can focus on the game." Shelby knew nothing about the game, but it gave her a good excuse to avoid Kenzi's prying gaze. If she continued dating Tucker though, she'd have to have him teach her the rules.

As she watched him run out on the field, she realized she was practically his date. Her. Shelby Doll. The woman who blended into the background was here as Tucker Jackson's guest, and hopefully, they'd be going on their first official date soon.

"What are you smirking about?" Kenzi asked, dispelling Shelby's daydream.

"Nothing. Just enjoying the game." And she did enjoy it. At least as much as she understood. She might not have known what each play was or exactly how the points were scored, but she knew to cheer every time the Tornadoes put points on the board. When the final whistle blew, they had secured a win by a mere three points. But a win was a win, right?

EPILOGUE

Seven Months Later

Tucker touched the box in his pocket to make sure it was still there. He'd spent a week shopping for the perfect ring, but had found nothing he liked. Thankfully, when he'd mentioned it to his father, whom he was now talking to on a regular basis, he'd suggested Tucker's mother's ring. The ring was simple and elegant - just like Shelby, and he couldn't wait to see the look on her face when he slid it on her finger. What better time than the re-opening of the center?

"You ready?" his father whispered in his ear.

Tucker still couldn't get over the change in his father. After the heart attack, his father had cut back on his case load. He'd begun spending more time with Whitley, and he'd even started attending church again where he'd met a wonderful woman, Meredith.

"Yeah, thanks again, Dad." Tucker smiled at his father, glad for their mended relationship.

"Good luck, big brother," Whitley said as she tossed him a wink before continuing into the center with his father and Meredith.

"What was that about?" Shelby asked as she rejoined him. She'd been conversing with her own family who was now following his family into the center.

"Nothing, just wishing us luck." He searched her face for any clue she might have guessed his intentions for tonight.

"Are you okay?" Her brow furrowed as she touched his arm.

"What?" He realized he was staring and shook his head. "Yes, I'm fine. Just excited to see what Kenzi's done with the place." After the Christmas party, Kenzi had realized she had a knack for decorating and had returned to college to work on her degree. The team, after seeing the center at the Christmas party, had agreed to donate a sizable amount of money to help renovate the center and hired Kenzi to head it. It had been a rush renovation because they couldn't close the center too long, but a local church had offered to let them use its building until the renovation was complete. Tonight would be the first time Shelby and Tucker would get to see the center.

"I'm sure she did an amazing job, but don't you think we're a little overdressed?" Her hand slid down the side of her dark blue evening gown as if she could smooth out the nerves she was feeling. Kenzi had planned a formal reveal. She'd gotten several wealthy families and business owners to attend by connecting the reveal to a donation dinner.

He turned to her and took her hands. "We're not overdressed, Shelby. This is a huge deal, and there are going to be a lot of eyes on you. You just need to remind yourself how amazing you are."

A soft pink glow raced across her cheeks, making her even more beautiful. "Thank you, Tucker. I just... I feel very out of my element."

"Hah, well now you know how I felt working at the center when I first started." He'd been completely out of his element, but he wouldn't change it for the world now. Not only had he met Shelby and the amazing kids, but he had learned to value the important things in life. Things like family and love. His hand touched his pocket again. He couldn't wait to propose to her.

Her shoulders rose and fell with her deep breath. Then she tossed him a smile and lifted her chin. "Okay, I'm ready."

Shelby could never have imagined the center looking as it

did now. The floor had been waxed and the walls redone. Instead of the sad faded cream walls, they were now filled with kids' artwork and exploded with color. The carpet in the office and hallways had been replaced as had the computer in the reception area. It almost looked like a brand new building.

Tables covered in white tablecloths filled the gym area, and decorative candles and flower arrangements added pops of color. As Shelby and Tucker entered, those already seated stood and began clapping. Shelby couldn't believe how many people Kenzi had managed to convince to come. Of course, she shouldn't have been surprised. Kenzi had the charming and persuasive personality.

"Here she is, the lady of the hour," Kenzi said from the front of the gym where a makeshift microphone had been set up. "Shelby, get up here and tell us about the new plans for the center."

Tucker squeezed her hand and planted a quick kiss on her lips before motioning her to the front. As she walked through the crowd, butterflies woke and took flight in her stomach. Speaking to large crowds of donors had always been nerve wracking to her.

Shelby took the mic and cleared her throat. "First, I just want to say thank you to everyone who came out tonight. Didn't Kenzi do an amazing job on the interior of this place?" Cheers and applause answered her question, giving Shelby the courage to continue.

"Well, thanks to a wonderful donation from the Texas Tornadoes, not only were we able to redecorate, but we've also created a collaborative program. Once a month, a football player will host a day here at the center to teach kids about exercise, teamwork, and of course football. This day will be free for all who are regular attenders at the center, and I'm pleased to announce that this program has brought in over fifty new children." Another round of clapping ensued.

"We'll be hiring a few full time staff members to help accommodate our new numbers as well as several part time members, allowing us not only to serve the kids but also bring jobs to the community. This couldn't have been possible without our very first volunteer, so would you please give a round of applause to Tucker Jackson?"

Shelby smiled as the cheers grew louder as Tucker approached the stage. She handed him the mic and moved to step back, but he caught her hand, holding her in place.

"Thank you, Shelby. I didn't know what to expect when I was first told I had to volunteer here, but I quickly learned that these kids had more to teach me than I could ever teach them. As did Shelby here. Many of you know that we've been dating for the last seven months. I would have been a fool not to pursue this amazing woman, but tonight you guys get to join in on what I hope will be our next step." He motioned to Kenzi who Shelby hadn't even noticed had been waiting off to the side. Then he handed her the mic.

Shelby's face clouded with confusion and then surprise as he reached into his pocket. He lowered to one knee and held out the box to her. As unobtrusively as possible, Kenzi held the mic so his words would carry as well. "Shelby, you changed my life the day I met you, and I can't imagine a day without you in it. Would you do me the honor of being my wife?"

He flicked open the box, and Shelby gasped and covered her mouth with her hands. Inside was the most beautiful ring she had ever seen. Tears blurred her eyes, and she was afraid no sound would come out of her mouth so she nodded. A cheer took over the place as he slipped the ring on her finger.

Though Shelby had prayed for a man, she had never expected God to send her one like Tucker Jackson. She supposed that just confirmed what she'd always known in her heart. God was an amazing, loving Father, and life worked out better when you let Him be in control.

The End!

IT'S NOT QUITE THE END!

Thank you so much for reading *Run With My Heart*. This book was inspired by my love of football and the amazing feedback I received on Her Second Chance Forever Groom.

I hope you enjoyed the story as I really enjoyed writing it. If you did, would you do me a favor? If you did, please leave a review. It really helps. It doesn't have to be long - just a few words to help other readers know what they're getting.

I'd love to hear from you, not only about this story, but about the characters or stories you'd like read in the future. I'm always looking for new ideas and if I use one of your characters or stories, I'll send you a free ebook and paperback of the book with a special dedication. Write to me at loranahoopes@gmail.com. And if you'd like to see what's coming next, be sure to stop by authorloranahoopes.com

I also have a weekly newsletter that contains many wonderful things like pictures of my adorable children, chances to win awesome prizes, new releases and sales I might be holding, great books from other authors, and anything else that strikes my fancy and that I think you would enjoy. I'll even send you the first chapter of my newest (maybe not even released yet) book if you'd like to sign up.

Even better, I solemnly swear to only send out one newsletter a week (usually on Tuesday unless life gets in the way which with three kids it usually does). I will not spam you, sell your email address to solicitors or anyone else, or any of those other terrible things.

God Bless,
Lorana

❦ 20 ❦

NOT READY TO SAY GOODBYE YET?

Run With My Heart is the first book in the Texas Tornado series. Continue the journey with Love on the Line - Blaine's story

Love on the Line

He's the quarterback who seems too good to be true.

She's the designer he's hired to redo his house.

But when she finds out his darkest secret, will it draw them together or tear them apart?

Click here to preorder Love on the Line

21

A FREE STORY FOR YOU

Enjoyed this story? Not ready to quit reading yet? If you sign up for my newsletter, you will receive The Billionaire's Impromptu Bet right away as my thank you gift for choosing to hang out with me.

The Billionaire's Impromptu Bet

A SWAT officer. A bored billionaire heiress. A bet that could change everything....

Read on for a taste of The Billionaire's Impromptu Bet....

22

THE BILLIONAIRE'S IMPROMPTU
BET PREVIEW

B rie Carter fell back spread eagle on her queen-sized canopy bed sending her blonde hair fanning out behind her. With a large sigh, she uttered, "I'm bored."

"How can you be bored? You have like millions of dollars." Her friend, Ariel, plopped down in a seated position on the bed beside her and flicked her raven hair off her shoulder. "You want to go shopping? I hear Tiffany's is having a special right now."

Brie rolled her eyes. Shopping? Where was the excitement in that? With her three platinum cards, she could go shopping whenever she wanted. "No, I'm bored with shopping too. I have everything. I want to do something exciting. Something we don't normally do."

Brie enjoyed being rich. She loved the unlimited credit

cards at her disposal, the constant apparel of new clothes, and of course the penthouse apartment her father paid for, but lately, she longed for something more fulfilling.

Ariel's hazel eyes widened. "I know. There's a new bar down on Franklin Street. Why don't we go play a little game?"

Brie sat up, intrigued at the secrecy and the twinkle in Ariel's eyes. "What kind of game?"

"A betting game. You let me pick out any man in the place. Then you try to get him to propose to you."

Brie wrinkled her nose. "But I don't want to get married." She loved her freedom and didn't want to share her penthouse with anyone, especially some man.

"You don't marry him, silly. You just get him to propose."

Brie bit her lip as she thought. It had been awhile since her last relationship and having a man dote on her for a month might be interesting, but.... "I don't know. It doesn't seem very nice."

"How about I sweeten the pot? If you win, I'll set you up on a date with my brother."

Brie cocked her head. Was she serious? The only thing Brie couldn't seem to buy in the world was the affection of Ariel's very handsome, very wealthy, brother. He was a movie star, just the kind of person Brie could consider marrying in the future. She'd had a crush on him as long as she and Ariel had been friends, but he'd always seen her as just that, his little sister's friend. "I thought you didn't want me dating your brother."

"I don't." Ariel shrugged. "But he's between girlfriends right now, and I know you've wanted it for ages. If you win this bet, I'll set you up. I can't guarantee any more than one date though. The rest will be up to you."

Brie wasn't worried about that. Charm she possessed in abundance. She simply needed some alone time with him, and she was certain she'd be able to convince him they were meant to be together. "All right. You've got a deal."

Ariel smiled. "Perfect. Let's get you changed then and see who the lucky man will be.

A tiny tug pulled on Brie's heart that this still wasn't right, but she dismissed it. This was simply a means to an end, and he'd never have to know.

Jesse Calhoun relaxed as the rhythmic thudding of the speed bag reached his ears. Though he loved his job, it was stressful being the SWAT sniper. He hated having to take human lives and today had been especially rough. The team had been called out to a drug bust, and Jesse was forced to return fire at three hostiles. He didn't care that they fired at his team and himself first. Taking a life was always hard, and every one of them haunted his dreams.

"You gonna bust that one too?" His co-worker Brendan appeared by his side. Brendan was the opposite of Jesse in nearly every way. Where Jesse's hair was a dark copper, Brendan's was nearly black. Jesse sported paler skin and a dusting of freckles across his nose, but Brendan's skin was naturally dark and freckle free.

Jesse flashed a crooked grin, but kept his eyes on the small, swinging black bag. The speed bag was his way to release, but a few times he had started hitting while still too keyed up and he had ruptured the bag. Okay, five times, but who was counting really? Besides, it was a better way to calm his nerves than other things he could choose. Drinking, fights, gambling, women.

"Nah, I think this one will last a little longer." His shoulders began to burn, and he gave the bag another few punches for good measure before dropping his arms and letting it swing to a stop. "See? It lives to be hit at least another day." Every once in a while, Jesse missed training the way he used to. Before he joined the force, he had been an amateur boxer, on his way to being a pro, but a shoulder injury had delayed his training and forced him to consider something else. It had eventually healed, but by then he had lost his edge.

"Hey, why don't you come drink with us?" Brendan

clapped a hand on Jesse's shoulder as they headed into the locker room.

"You know I don't drink." Jesse often felt like the outsider of the team. While half of the six-man team was married, the other half found solace in empty bottles and meaningless relationships. Jesse understood that - their job was such that they never knew if they would come home night after night - but he still couldn't partake.

Brendan opened his locker and pulled out a clean shirt. He peeled off his current one and added deodorant before tugging on the new one. "You don't have to drink. Look, I won't drink either. Just come and hang out with us. You have no one waiting for you at home."

That wasn't entirely true. Jesse had Bugsy, his Boston Terrier, but he understood Brendan's point. Most days, Jesse went home, fed Bugsy, made dinner, and fell asleep watching TV on the couch. It wasn't much of a life. "All right, I'll go, but I'm not drinking."

Brendan's lips pulled back to reveal his perfectly white teeth. He bragged about them, but Jesse knew they were veneers. "That's the spirit. Hurry up and change. We don't want to leave the rest of the team waiting."

"Is everyone coming?" Jesse pulled out his shower necessities. Brendan might feel comfortable going out with just a new application of deodorant, but Jesse needed to wash more than just dirt and sweat off. He needed to wash the sound of the bullets and the sight of lifeless bodies from his mind.

"Yeah, Pat's wife is pregnant again and demanding some crazy food concoctions. Pat agreed to pick them up if she let him have an hour. Cam and Jared's wives are having a girls' night, so the whole gang can be together. It will be nice to hang out when we aren't worried about being shot at."

"Fine. Give me ten minutes. Unlike you, I like to clean up before I go out."

Brendan smirked. "I've never had any complaints. Besides, do you know how long it takes me to get my hair like this?"

Jesse shook his head as he walked into the shower, but he knew it was true. Brendan had rugged good looks and muscles to match. He rarely had a hard time finding a woman. Jesse on the other hand hadn't dated anyone in the last few months. It wasn't that he hadn't been looking, but he was quieter than his teammates. And he wasn't looking for right now. He was looking for forever. He just hadn't found it yet.

Click here to continue reading The Billionaire's Impromptu Bet.

THE STORY DOESN'T END!

You've met a few people and fallen in love....

I bet you're wondering how you can meet everyone else.

Star Lake Series:

When Love Returns: Can Presley and Brandon forget past hurts or will their stubborn natures keep them apart forever?

Once Upon a Star: Now that Blake has gained confidence and some muscle, will he finally be able to reveal his feelings to Audrey?

Love Conquers All: Now that Azarius has another chance with Laney, will he find the courage to share his life with her? Or will his emotional walls create a barrier that will leave him alone once more?

The Heartbeats Series:

Where It All Began: Will Sandra tell Henry her darkest secret? And will she ever be able to forgive herself and find healing? Find out in this emotional love story.

The Power of Prayer: Who will Callie choose and how will her choice affect the rest of her life? Find out in this touching novel.

When Hearts Collide: Amanda captivates his heart, but can Jared save her from making the biggest mistake of her life? A must read for mothers and daughters.

A Past Forgiven: Can Chad leave his bad-boy image behind and step up and be there for Jess and the baby?

Sweet Billionaires Series:

The Billionaire's Secret: Can Max really change his philandering ways? Or will one mistake seal his fate forever?

A Brush with a Billionaire: Will Brent and Sam's stubborn natures keep them apart or can a small town festival bring them together?

The Billionaire's Christmas Miracle: Drew Devonshire is captivated by the woman he meets at a masquerade ball, but who is she?

The Billionaire's Cowboy Groom: When Carrie returns to town requesting a divorce, can he convince her they belong together?

The Cowboy Billionaire: Coming Soon!

The Lawkeeper Series:

Lawfully Matched: Will Jesse find his fiancee's

killer? And when Kate flies into his life, will he be able to put his painful past behind him in order to love again?

Lawfully Justified: Can Emma offer William a reason to stay? Can William find a way to heal from his broken past to start a future with Emma? Or will a haunting secret take away all the possibilities of this budding romance?

The Scarlet Wedding: William and Emma are planning their wedding, but an outbreak and a return from his past force them to change their plans. Is a happily ever after still in their future?

Lawfully Redeemed: Dani Higgins is a K9 cop looking to make a name for herself, but she finds herself at the mercy of a stranger after an accident. Calvin Phillips just wanted to help his brother, but somehow he ended up in the middle of a police investigation and caring for the woman trying to bring his brother in.

The Still Small Voice Series:

The Still Small Voice: Will Kat be able to give up control and do what God is asking of her?

A Spark in the Darkness coming soon!

Blushing Brides Series:

The Cowboy's Reality Bride: Laney Swann has been running from her past for years, but it takes meeting a man on a reality dating show to make her see there's no need to run.

The Reality Bride's Baby: Laney wants nothing

more than a baby, but when she starts feeling dizzy is it pregnancy or something more serious?

The Producer's Unlikely Bride: Ava McDermott is waiting for the perfect love, but after agreeing to a fake relationship with Justin, she finds herself falling for real.

Ava's Blessing in Disguise: Five years after marriage, Ava faces a mysterious illness that threatens to ruin her career. Will she find out what it is?

The Soldier's Steadfast Bride: coming soon

The Men of Fire Beach

Fire Games: Cassidy returns home from Who Wants to Marry a Cowboy to find obsessive letters from a fan. The cop assigned to help her wants to get back to his case, but what she sees at a fire may just be the key he's looking for.

Lost Memories and New Beginnings: She has no idea who she is. He's the doctor caring for her. When her past collides with his present, can he keep her safe?

When Questions Abound A companion story to Lost Memories, this book tells the story from Detective Jordan Graves's point of view.

Never Forget the Past

Secrets and Suspense coming soon!

Stand Alones:

Love Renewed: This books is part of the multi author second chance series. When fate reunites high school sweethearts separated by life's choices, can they find a second chance at love at a snowy lodge amid a little mystery?

Her children's early reader chapter book series:

The Wishing Stone #1: Dangerous Dinosaur

The Wishing Stone #2: Dragon Dilemma

The Wishing Stone #3: Mesmerizing Mermaids

The Wishing Stone #4: Pyramid Puzzle

The Wishing Stone Inspirations 1: Mary's Miracle

To see a list of all her books

authorloranahoopes.com

loranahoopes@gmail.com

DISCUSSION QUESTIONS

1. What was your favorite scene in the book? What made it your favorite?

2. Did you have a favorite line in the book? What do you think made it so memorable?

3. Who was your favorite character in the book and why?

4. Tucker faced anger issues in the book. Do you think they were justified?

5. What do you think would be the hardest part about dating a celebrity?

6. What did you learn about God from reading this book?

7. How can you use that knowledge in your life from now on?

8. What can you take away from Shelby and Tucker's relationship?

9. What do you think would make the story even better?

ABOUT THE AUTHOR

Lorana Hoopes is an inspirational author originally from Texas but now living in the PNW with her husband and three children. When not writing, she can be seen kick-boxing at the gym, singing, or acting on stage. One day, she hopes to retire from teaching and write full time.

www.ingramcontent.com/pod-product-compliance
Lightning Source LLC
Chambersburg PA
CBHW030305200626
46816CB00002BA/766